Murder With a Hint of PEPPERMINT

LAURA M. DRAKE

WHISPER HOLLOW MYSTERIES
BOOK 2

Acknowledgements

Thank you to my family and friends who support me, the readers who make this job worth doing, and everyone who loved Murder With a Hint of Pumpkin Spice so much that I couldn't wait to get the sequel published.

Contents

1. Christmas in Whisper Hollow   1

2. UnEXpected Encounters   14

3. The Accidental Boyfriend   25

4. Breaking the Curse   33

5. Ghosts of Christmas Past   42

6. Deadly Alibis   52

7. Tangled in Tinsel and Lies   61

8. Making a List and Checking it Twice   73

9. Tying the Knot   85

10. Mistletoe and Murderers   95

11. Claus on Pause   104

12. All I Want for Christmas is a Not-Fake Boyfriend   116

13. Kiss Me S'more   124

14. This Christmas I'll Give You My Heart   137

15. Naughty or Nice   149

16. Silent Night, Deadly Night   157

17. Run Rudolph Run   166

18. Best Christmas Ever   176

19. New Year's Resolutions   184

About the author   188

Also by   189

Afterword   191

Book Club Questions   192

Laura M. Drake's QR Code   194

Chapter 1

Christmas in Whisper Hollow

"Christmas is the perfect time for murder," I told María as I shelved more books in the mystery section of my bookshop, Whispering Pages.

The soft sounds of "Silver Bells" playing from Nana's gramophone partially covered María's snort. "What are you talking about, Harper? People don't want murders in December. They want mistletoe and romance and ice skating and hot chocolate."

I flicked the fluffy white ball hanging on the end of her Santa cap and shelved a Sherlock Holmes book. "Then why are my mysteries selling so well—especially the cozy murders?"

"That's the true mystery here." She took another sip of her cinnamon spice tea. "Besides, what's cozy about a murder, anyway? That adjective is entirely inaccurate."

"You're such a fantasy snob. Nothing else is good enough." I grinned at her and straightened the row of Christmas lights I'd strung across the bookshelves. "Good thing I've got a large fantasy section."

"I guess you have me to thank for that, don't you?" María grinned and adjusted her hat over her dark curls.

"Because you helped me save the bookshop?"

She laughed and picked up one of the sparkly store-bought snowflakes that had fallen to the floor. I'd hung a blizzard of them across the ceiling. "Not at all. Your grandmother's money saved the store. I meant you could thank me for trying to buy out your fantasy section single-handedly."

"And that's why we're friends. Grace never gets my nerdy fantasy references." I smiled and elbowed her in the side. "And also because your Halloween party helped save the store."

"Well, that's true. My parties are fantastic."

"That's not the only thing." I straightened a garland of pine, holly, and red berries decorating the windowsill, then some fake snow on top of the tiny Christmas village I'd pulled from storage. Nana's seasonal decorations were out of control ... and I sort of loved it. "I've also had a lot of new people come in, thanks to your Christmas Wish idea."

Hiring María as my marketer after Kyle quit his part-time job was one of the best decisions I'd made since taking over the bookshop.

María beamed and gathered from the front desk all the paper stars decorated with glitter we'd cut and threaded with string. When customers came in, they could write a gift for someone who couldn't afford it on a star or take a filled-out star from the tree if they wanted to buy a gift for someone. "Wishing Stars were popular where I grew up, and I thought it would be fun to do it here too."

"It's been great."

"I'm looking forward to the Christmas Festival." I helped her hang them on the towering tree in the corner, then stepped back to admire the flashing lights, tinsel, and ornaments.

"Me too." María glanced at the snowman-shaped advent calendar on the front desk but didn't open the flap yet. We'd do that in the morning. "Because the Christmas Festival happens two days before Christmas, it feels like Christmas lasts for forty-eight hours. It's the best—sort of like celebrating my birthday all week long."

The door jingled as someone came in, and María sighed.

"Welcome to Whispering Pages, where every book has a story to tell." I smiled at the lanky man standing by the door in a puffy black jacket. Even when customers came in five minutes before closing, I was still grateful for sales. "What can I help you with?"

María went around doing some of the other, less conspicuous closing procedures in a not-so-subtle hint for him to leave.

"I'm looking for a gift for my girlfriend." He pushed his glasses up his nose, then did a double-take at me. "Have we met?"

"I don't think so." I shrugged.

"Weird." He shook his head. His blond hair stuck out around his ears from under his beanie.

I exchanged a confused glance with María, who gave me a look that said *I think he's flirting with you.* I waved her off and gestured to the Christmas books on display on the front table. "Would your girlfriend enjoy a holiday read?"

"I'm not sure."

"Is she a fantasy lover?" I gestured to the fantasy section, where a small Father Christmas with a long white beard stood guard. I'd placed him there since he reminded me of Gandalf the White.

"Maybe?" The man cocked his head to the side.

"How about romance? We have some fun holiday reads." I walked to another display and picked up a book. "This one is quite popular. It has a love triangle and—"

"No. No love triangles." His shoulders tensed and he rubbed his forehead.

"Okay." I put the book down and moved to a different section. "How about murder mysteries?" I grinned at María over his shoulder, and she stuck her tongue out at me behind the man's back.

"She might be interested in that." His brow furrowed, and he let out a self-deprecating laugh. "Now that I'm here, I'm realizing I have no idea what sort of book she likes. I just wanted to do something to help—to surprise her. I'll come back tomorrow once I have more information." With that, he left the shop as abruptly as he came.

"*That* was weird, but *this* is cute. I can't believe I didn't notice it before." María held up a glass decoration shaped like an open book. A miniature quill rested across the pages, as if waiting for someone to pick it up and finish writing the lines etched into the page.

My heart thumped, remembering the Christmas Tate gave it to me, but I just shrugged. "Yeah, it fits the theme, so I put it out." Part of me wanted to throw it, and all the memories it represented, away, but the rest of me recognized how adorable it was. I was perfectly capable of keeping a memento from someone I hadn't seen in ten months without letting it affect me. "You ready to go?"

"Right." María linked her arm through mine and tugged me toward the door. She plucked off her Santa hat and put it back on a snowman's head. "It's time for your hot date with Sebastian."

"It isn't a date." I laughed and straightened the book wreath hanging on the inside of the door. It was one of my favorite decorations, since Nana and I had made it together when I was a little girl. We'd created it from pages of old books, then wrapped it with a festive red bow.

"What else do you call dinner with an attractive man you *would* date in a heartbeat?"

I flushed and avoided her gaze while I grabbed my key to lock the door, then I set the alarm on my phone. After what happened to Mr. James a few months ago, I wasn't taking any more chances. "I call it dinner with a friend."

"I need more friends like that." María turned off the lights, though it didn't hide her smirk. "Although you're a fool if all you want is friendship."

"I didn't say that was all I wanted, just that it's how it is right now. It's probably for the best, anyway." Considering Sebastian had mentioned an ex at dinner a few weeks ago, I was pretty sure he wasn't over her, which took the pressure off our friendship. Then there was the fact that I also didn't feel ready to jump back into dating or risk ruining our friendship.

We pulled on our coats and stepped into the biting December wind. Although it was only six-thirty, the sky was dark and ominous in contrast to the fresh snow that covered the ground from the afternoon. Christmas lights illuminated Main Street and glittered off the blanket of white.

Out on the icy sidewalk, a man bumped into me as I locked up and walked off with a muttered, "Sorry."

The faint acrid smell emanating from him dragged my thoughts back to Tate, who'd quit smoking after we'd started dating. Realizing, I was thinking of Tate, I wrinkled my nose and focused back on María.

"... and *you're* ridiculous if you think anyone is buying this whole 'friend' thing," she said.

A couple exited through the door of Sugarplum Delights, flooding the street with the delicious aroma of freshly baked bread and cinnamon and making my stomach rumble.

"I'm serious," I insisted. Even if I wanted to be more than friends, how could it possibly work after everything we'd been through? Between my pepper-spraying him on our first meeting, my cat ruining his work project, and my accidentally blaming him for murder, it was hard to believe we'd made it to friendship. I frowned at the thought. Looking back put everything in embarrassing clarity. All the complications in our relationship were distinctly one-sided.

"I'm just saying that meeting someone of the opposite sex every week for dinner sounds an awful lot like a date." María peered through the display window of Sugarplum Delights, and the smile fell from her face. "On second thought, maybe I was wrong."

Ignoring the artfully arranged pinecones, miniature ornaments, and fake snow in Nancy's display window, I searched for what had caused María's sudden mood shift.

My gaze was drawn to Sebastian like I was Harry and he was the Mirror of Erised. He sat at our usual table with his strong, callused hands wrapped around a steaming mug that was probably peppermint tea—something I'd learned was his favorite. I studied his profile from the street, the messy chestnut hair and strong jaw.

He smiled at something, and an answering smile pulled at my lips.

At least until someone leaned across the table, and a feminine, well-manicured hand rested on his bicep. The hand was attached to an attractive brunette in an infuriatingly adorable Christmas sweater.

Sebastian was at Sugarplum Delights, but he appeared to be on a date.

And the worst part was: it wasn't with me.

I stared through the frosted window at the woman. She touched Sebastian's arm again and threw her head back in a laugh.

Who even laughed like that?

My thoughts darted to when I'd discovered Tate and Ashley together, and I shoved the memory away. The situation with Sebastian wasn't even remotely similar to what had happened before—we weren't even dating—so why would it make me think of that?

María placed a gentle hand on my back. "Are you okay?"

I tore my gaze from the window to find her studying me. "Okay? Of course, I'm okay. Why wouldn't I be?"

Her dark eyes filled with sympathy. "Maybe because Sebastian is with another woman, and you look like you're ready to Fernand Mondego her?"

I turned away from the brunette who was touching Sebastian's arm again. "You mean the guy from *The Count of Monte Cristo* who tried to kill Edmond?"

"The one who tried to kill him because he was jealous." She drew out the last word.

"Don't be ridiculous. I'm not jealous, and I'm not going to kill her." I stepped back and shook my head. "Sebastian is more than welcome to eat dinner with anyone he wants." Our plans tonight had been more on the unstated-but-understood side of things. At least I thought they'd been understood since we'd been meeting every week for a while. After bumping into each other a few times at the bakery, we'd ended up sharing a meal, and that meal had led to another the next week, and the next, until we were meeting for dinner at Nancy's at least once a week. But seeing him with that woman reminded me that we didn't have any real plans together, and I had no right to ruin his dinner.

"If you're not jealous, then should we join them?"

"No." Sitting there watching someone flirt with Sebastian sounded about as appealing as snaking the toilet. And considering the way he'd smiled at her, he hardly needed rescuing.

María looped her arm through mine. "Want to come over to my place? We could watch a movie or something to get your mind off it."

I forced a laugh but let her lead me away from the bakery. Our footsteps crunched in the snow. "I don't need to get my mind off of it. I'm fine."

"Uh-huh." She glanced over her shoulder. "You know, I think Helen has been causing quite a bit of drama in town."

"Who is Helen?" Unlike her, I refused to look back.

"The woman with Sebastian." She gave me a *duh* look like I should've figured that out already. "I'm not surprised you haven't met her yet though. She doesn't usually visit Nancy's. Anyway, remember the guy who came in before closing?"

"Yeah."

"That's Tom. He and Helen are dating—or sort of dating—which is weird since it felt like he was hitting on you earlier. But maybe it makes sense since I've heard she's been sniffing around Sebastian." María shrugged and pulled her coat tighter against the brisk wind. "There's been gossip all around town, but I didn't put much stock into it until now. Maybe their relationship is on the rocks."

So, she was cheating on her boyfriend? Or maybe not, if they weren't officially dating. Still, though, I knew there was a reason I didn't like her. "All around town or just in Sugarplum Delights?" I asked. "Because you sound like you've been talking to Nancy."

"Maybe a bit. I live off of Nancy's coffee and gossip." María flashed a smile at me. "It's like watching a train wreck. I can't help wondering who she'll go for next. She goes after men like a lioness going in for the kill."

We made it to the alley that led to the small parking lot behind the shop. I stopped and extricated my arm from María's. "Thanks for the invite, but I think I'll head home. I've got some stuff to do."

"Yeah, I totally believe you." She shook her head, and her silky dark hair moved around her shoulders. "Well, if you change your mind, you know where I live."

Another blast of wintry air hit me as I followed the tracks in the snow people had left before me. I shivered and folded my arms across my chest for warmth. This was why I'd stopped biking for the winter.

The sight of Helen's hand on Sebastian's arm flashed through my mind, and I shook my head and blew out a frustrated breath. It puffed in front of me in a blast of white that quickly dissipated in the frigid air.

Laughter sounded in the street behind me, pulling me from my thoughts and emphasizing how silent the alley was. The hairs on my neck stood on end, and I couldn't shake the creeping sensation that I wasn't alone. The lights from Main Street couldn't penetrate the thick shadows clinging to the alley, leaving me walking through a twenty-foot stretch of gloom.

Footsteps sounded behind me. It could've been from someone on the street, but somehow I didn't think so. It was too deliberate. Too slow. Too close.

A surge of fear propelled me forward as dread gnawed at my insides. My footsteps drummed a frantic beat on the pavement to match my racing heart.

I stole a glance over my shoulder but couldn't make out anything in the dim lighting.

When I made it to my car, I let out a tense breath, unlocked it with shaking hands, then slipped inside. I locked the doors and peered into the alley again, but nothing moved in the gloom.

I let out a tense laugh, remembering how Jiji had scared me in the alley back in October. Clearly, I hadn't learned my lesson since I'd let myself get freaked out for no reason. I'd obviously been wrong about the footsteps after all.

After putting in my AirPod, I called Grace, who answered on the third ring.

"It's not like you to call right now," she said. Ever since she and her family had come out in November to celebrate when Nancy, Sebastian, and I split the purchase and officially bought the building that housed our shops, she'd been even more invested in my life in Whisper Hollow than ever before. "Did your dinner with Sebastian end early?"

"I suppose you could say that," I grumbled.

"Did Sebastian bail on your date?"

"It isn't a date," I repeated for what already felt like the millionth time. Even still, he could've told me he had other plans.

"I see." Her tone made me feel like she really did see—and probably far too much. "Did you at least call him to find out why? Maybe something came up tonight."

I rolled my eyes and turned the heater on full blast as I drove home. "Oh, something definitely came up. He was with another woman."

"He was?"

Her surprise was as obvious to me as my discontent must've been to her. Darn sister-bond.

"Yes." I spent the rest of my short drive home explaining what had happened. It was a pretty short story, but my frustration helped me drag it out. I pulled into the driveway. A soft, golden light from the Christmas tree spilled through the curtained windows, casting a warm and inviting glow on the snow around the house. I'd programmed the tree here, and at the shop, to be on a timer so the Christmas lights could always welcome me back.

"Well, that sucks. I thought for sure he was into you."

"You did?" I unlocked the front door and opened it. The scent of pine from the wreath on the door greeted me, along with an anxious meow.

"Yeah, it seemed pretty obvious." She mumbled something to one of her kids that sounded like "no desserts before dinner," then, "About as obvious as you being into him."

"I'm not into him!" I lied. "Besides, you know I'm not ready to be with someone, Grace."

She tsked and I could practically see her shaking her head. "Just because you aren't ready for a boyfriend, doesn't mean you don't like Sebastian."

"Maybe." Being over Tate's betrayal and being ready to hand my heart to someone else were two very different things.

"So, what now?"

"Now, nothing." I leaned down to pet Jiji, who wrapped around my legs like a pair of furry black socks. After straightening, I let the lights from the Christmas tree in the living room guide me down the front hall and onto the couch, where I curled up with one of Nana's throws. "I'm going to eat some leftovers and read."

Grace groaned. "Oh no. I'm sensing some serious regressing happening here. We're back to fantasy novels on a Friday night?"

"Just because I'm single doesn't mean you can guilt-trip me into spending every weekend being social." I glared at the pillow on my lap, which wasn't nearly as effective as glaring at Grace would've been. "I deserve a night to myself now and then."

Jiji hopped onto my lap and kneaded her claws in the blanket before curling up on me and giving a contented meow.

"Jiji agrees that I deserve a night at home," I added.

Grace sighed. "The problem isn't that you're having a Me Night *tonight*. It's that every other night, except for your dinners with Sebastian, is a Me Night. And also that you're talking for your cat."

"Whatever. Sometimes I hang with María or Jessie." I petted Jiji, whose body thrummed with a contented purr. The lights from the tree glinted off the tiny snow village decorating the top of the fireplace mantle and the tinsel along the window. The buildings all had the same peaked, snow-covered roofs and bright windows, placing them in the same set as the building at Whispering Pages. So many of these decorations brought back memories of Nana with a pang.

"True," Grace agreed. "I'm glad Nana forced you to interact with them on that scavenger hunt. They've been good friends."

"Hey, I met María on my own, thank you very much." Technically, she came into the store, but Grace didn't need to know that.

Grace laughed. "Fine, fine. So how is your Christmas Wish thing going?"

"Great. We've had tons of people participate, and I've had to move presents from under the tree back to my office to make more space."

"That's nice that you're doing that, Harp."

"I feel like I should pay it forward after how blessed I was to be able to buy Whispering Pages, ya know? I want to help María make this a success." Plus, focusing on the Christmas Wish program helped me not feel so alone during the holidays.

I stretched and knocked some of the tinsel to the ground. Trying not to dislodge Jiji—because once a cat was on you, you couldn't get up again—I reached for the tinsel and replaced it on the windowsill. I turned slightly to tweak it at the end, and something in the snow caught my eye.

"How odd," I mumbled as I pressed my forehead against the chilled glass to look more closely. Jiji gave a disgruntled meow and cracked one eye open to glare at me.

"What's odd?"

"There are footprints outside my window that weren't there this morning." I squinted to make out any additional details as the frozen chill of the glass seeped into me. A set of footprints appeared from the darkness and forayed into the snow outside my living room window as if someone had stood outside and peered in.

"And?" Grace said.

"And I didn't make them."

Chapter 2

UnEXpected Encounters

Whenever I had downtime at work the next day, my thoughts drifted to the strange footprints by my window. Unwilling to go outside by myself at night after freaking out in the alley, I'd waited until my run this morning to check the tracks, but a few inches of fresh powder hid the trail. Instead, I found a piece of shimmering blue plastic partially buried in the snow. It looked like some sort of wrapper with a bit of red in the corner. Maybe it had fallen out of the pocket of whoever had stood outside my window.

My phone buzzed with a text, so I pulled it out and read a message from Grace.

Have you talked to Sebastian yet?

No.

He'd texted me last night asking where I was, but all I'd told him was that I couldn't make it, after all.

The bell at the front door jingled, and I slipped my phone back into my pocket. "Welcome to Whispering Pages where every book has a story to tell," I called to the two men who walked in one after the other.

Outside, a police car rushed down Main Street, heading east. Its siren cut through the air like a cry for help, and the giant snowflake projections dancing across the building on the other side of the street turned red and blue from its lights as it sped by.

Where were they headed in such a hurry? Usually, the town was so sleepy and quiet. The siren's shrill ring faded in the distance as the car disappeared around the corner, but it left behind a lingering sense of unease that hung in the air.

Shaking off my strange thoughts, I turned back to my customers. The first, a redhead with a thick beard who appeared to be around my age, was standing by the display table reading the blurb from *A Christmas Carol* while the second, a middle-aged man with short brown hair partially hidden under a bowler hat, browsed the murder mystery section.

Too bad María wasn't here to see. I smirked to myself but kept a polite smile on. "Can I help you find anything?"

"Just looking around," the older gentleman said while the redhead shook his head without looking up from the book.

"Okay. Let me know if you need anything." I picked up the decorative snowflakes that had fallen from the ceiling—maybe stringing them up had been a bad idea—and tried not to wrinkle my nose at the smell of cigarette smoke one of the men had brought into the shop.

With only a few days until Christmas, customers had been trickling in all morning to buy last-minute gifts.

Half an hour later, the bell rang again and I glanced up. "Oh hey, Sebastian."

His dark chestnut hair was ruffled from the wind and his blue eyes narrowed. "Are you okay?"

"I'm fine." I straightened my spine and tried to sound casual and completely unfazed.

Sebastian's presence filled the air with electricity as noticeable as a summer storm. "I thought we were meeting at Nancy's last night."

The middle-aged man left, but the redhead continued browsing the Christmas books, apparently oblivious to the tension crackling through the room.

"Me too." I shouldn't have said that. I bit my lip and turned away to tidy some already-straight books on a shelf. "But you seemed busy."

He paused, and I wished I was turned around to try to read his expression, but then it'd make my own too obvious.

"So, you came."

"Just for a bit, but then I headed home to do some ... stuff." I winced at my terrible excuse. I sounded about as pathetic as I felt.

Sebastian walked over and leaned one hand on the bookshelf next to me. "What sort of stuff?"

I could feel him studying my face, and I flushed. Curse him for making me nervous and for being close enough to notice my embarrassment. I hurried to come up with something besides "snuggling Jiji" or "rereading *The Chronicles of Narnia*," but it wasn't easy.

"Christmas Festival prep," I finally said.

The redhead finally looked up, and his gaze darted between Sebastian and me before he put the book down with a muttered, "I'll come back later."

"Harp, listen to me," Sebastian said after the door closed again. "Whatever you saw last night. It wasn't anything. I was ambushed at the table."

"You didn't look ambushed," I mumbled as I readjusted a string of lights hanging across the shelf.

Sebastian moved his hand to my shoulder, and even through my thick sweater, I could feel the warmth from his touch. It worsened my blush and sent butterflies flapping around my stomach.

"I was trying to be friendly, since *someone* told me I wasn't approachable."

I stifled a smile, remembering a discussion we'd had a few weeks ago about our rocky introduction. I never would've lectured Sebastian about it had I known the moment he dropped his prickly guard, he'd be swarmed by females.

"But I was waiting for you to come and rescue me."

Jiji slunk out from my office and wrapped around his ankles.

"Very damsel in distress of you." I finally turned and met his gaze with a small smile. Now that I faced him, we were almost chest-to-chest.

His attention dropped to my lips. If it weren't for the fact that he had over six inches on me, our mouths would be close enough to lean in and touch.

My heart took off.

"I want you to know that I left Nancy's on my own last night and spent the rest of the night by myself since someone skipped dinner."

"I'm sorry," I said breathlessly, though my heart jumped a little hearing he'd left Helen behind.

The chime over the door jingled, breaking the spell.

I let out a breath and glanced away from Sebastian's magnetic gaze to the new customers.

A group of older ladies descended on the romance books in the corner like a pack of vultures in knit cardigans.

Sebastian stepped back and gave me a small smile. "Shall we try again tonight?"

"Yeah." My voice came out a little too breathless, so I cleared my throat and smoothed a hand down my skirt. "That sounds good." It sounded *good*? Was that the best I could do?

"I'll wait for you at Nancy's." He walked back to the door and called over his shoulder with a half-grin, "Try not to run away this time. Someone's going to have to rescue me if I'm in trouble again."

I shook my head and turned my attention to the customers.

"I can't believe you put off your Christmas shopping for so long," a woman with beautiful silver hair said to someone in her posse.

"I still have time." Another woman with white hair and bright red lipstick picked up a book and stared at the cover—a heaving bosom and ripped stomach under the words *Ho, Ho, Hoe*. A shockingly popular holiday romance that I would never be caught dead reading. She plucked a Christmas Wish from the tree, then brought them both to me. "How do I do this?"

"You buy whatever toy or gift is written on the front, then wrap it and drop it off here and we'll have Santa deliver it on Christmas Eve." I showed her the toy written on the front. "They vary in price depending on how many items are listed and if it's food, clothing, or toys. Make sure to keep the tag with it so we know which family it goes to."

"Perfect." She slipped the star into her overly-large handbag and paid for the book.

I gestured to a stack of empty stars on the front desk. "You can also fill one out if you know of anyone who needs something they can't afford, including presents for their children."

"I'll keep that in mind," she said as the rest of the women joined her at the desk.

"What a beautiful cat you have." The white-haired lady reached to pet Jiji, who decided to be a jerk and hop off the desk and stalk away with her tail in the air. The woman pouted and dropped her hand.

"Sorry about that. She can be a bit of a pill sometimes." I rang up all their steamy romance books and walked them to the door. "Thanks for coming."

A steady stream of customers kept me busy for the rest of the afternoon, but that didn't stop me from glancing at the clock too many times. After helping the final customers, I hurriedly closed up the store for the night and walked over to Sugarplum Delights.

Sebastian smiled at me from our table in the corner and gestured to the two steaming bowls in front of him. "I ordered dinner."

I slid into the seat next to him and raised my eyebrow. "Not that Nancy has bad food, but I hope you chose better than last time." Not that there was anything wrong with the pasta Nancy had made. Sebastian just hadn't known that I didn't like cherry tomatoes, but now he did.

Nancy bustled over, her face as soft and round as her shortbread cookies. "You're darn right, I don't have any bad food. I've trained my new help well."

"I'm glad," Sebastian said. "You needed more help. You were always working."

"But your food is as fantastic as ever, just like your decorations." I smiled and gestured to the poinsettias that provided a bright splash of red to contrast the green tablecloths and gold place settings.

"Christmas is by far my favorite season." She chuckled. "I think I even have a Santa suit lying around somewhere from back when I used to make George dress up."

"Well, your shop and your baked goods look amazing as always."

"You haven't seen anything yet." She lowered her voice to a conspiratorial whisper. "Wait until you see the edible Christmas tree I'm working on for the festival."

I laughed. "I'm looking forward to it."

"Not as much as I'm looking forward to hearing about last night." She gave Sebastian a pointed stare. "Seems like you had the wrong partner for dinner."

Sebastian ducked his head in an adorably abashed gesture. "You saw what happened. I was ambushed."

"I know." Nancy sighed. "Helen needs to get things figured out. I'm not sure she realizes how her actions can hurt others."

"Yeah, she can be quite ... determined when she wants to be," Sebastian said.

"That girl's going to leave a trail of broken hearts around town if she isn't careful." Nancy tsked and shook her head, then went to welcome another group of customers.

"You know the rules: buyer gets to choose, and no complaints." Sebastian smirked, bringing out the single dimple in his left cheek. "Tonight is butternut squash soup. Plus, Nancy's famous honey pepper bacon, of course."

I raised my water in acknowledgment. "Of course." Nancy's bacon was his favorite and he ordered it every week.

"I would never complain." A swirl of cream decorated the center of the orange-gold soup. One sip proved the flavor was smooth, velvety, and thick with a hint of caramelized sweetness and something like cinnamon or nutmeg.

"Yes, you just share your possibly critical opinions in detail," he said dryly. "You're like Bilbo Baggins with his penchant for good food. Or maybe that's a hobbit thing in general."

"You're such a nerd," I teased. "Who brings up hobbits at dinner?"

"Probably someone who's talking to someone whose favorite book is *The Hobbit*."

My chest tightened. He remembered that? It was something I'd mentioned once at least a month ago. "What can I say? I'm a woman who knows what she likes." I quickly took a bite of my food, my thoughts flashing back to how close we'd stood earlier. My food slid down the wrong pipe, and I choked.

Sebastian pounded on my back. "Are you okay?"

"I'm fine," I said despite my watering eyes. I took a drink of water, then inhaled slowly to calm the flutter in my chest. "Anyway, how was your day?"

"A lot better than yesterday."

"Oh?" I looked up at him, wishing I could do the single eyebrow raise he was so good at. "What happened?"

"Someone at the nursing home got mad at me yesterday."

I imagined one of the elderly ladies chasing after Sebastian with her cane, and a giggle burst from me. "As amusing as that thought is, I find it hard to believe. They all love you."

"Not everyone." He shook his head, and some of his dark hair flopped into his eyes.

My fingers twitched with the desire to smooth it back. Instead, I ate another bite of soup. If I was patient, I'd learned that Sebastian would fill in the details for me.

"A male employee was ticked at me for 'stealing his girl,' and that was *before* she crashed my dinner." He rolled his eyes. "Apparently, Helen's boyfriend doesn't appreciate her spending time with me."

"That makes two of us," I mumbled, but it was easier to brush off the Helen incident now than it had been last night.

"Three really."

"I wonder why she's so into you." The words were out before I fully thought them through. "Not that that's hard to believe."

Sebastian's grin widened.

"It's weird to eat dinner with you if she has a boyfriend."

The humor fled from his expression. "I made the mistake of standing up for her once when I noticed them getting into a fight at the nursing home, and I think it gave her the wrong impression."

Sebastian would do that.

"Anyway, Tom started yelling at me in the middle of the lobby at the nursing home."

"Ouch." I wrinkled my nose, trying to imagine the soft-spoken man who'd come into the bookshop yesterday doing that. I guess the rumors María had mentioned about Helen sniffing around Sebastian had reached him too. I couldn't decide if it was impressive or weird that he'd still come into the shop to get her a present despite knowing what she was doing, although that explained his 'no love triangles' comment. "That sounds unpleasant."

"From what I heard, it isn't his first time being involved in a scene at work."

I leaned closer. "What happened?"

"A few months ago, a patient under Tom's care died, and I guess the family blamed him. One of the other nurses got involved too, but I didn't get all the details. Sounds like it got pretty ugly though."

"Wow. Sounds intense. My day sounds peaceful in comparison." As long as I didn't count how frustrated I'd been with Sebastian all day until his appearance at the bookshop.

He finished his soup—he was always so much faster than me—and leaned across the table. "So how is the festival prep coming?"

"Festival prep?" I repeated, somewhat caught off guard by his proximity. Sebastian had a way of giving me his whole attention when we talked that made me feel like it was just him and me in the room.

"Yeah." He smiled slightly again, revealing the dimple that meant he was sort of laughing at me. The spark of amusement in his gaze matched the twinkling fairy lights Nancy had strung across the ceiling's exposed wooden beams. "You said you worked on stuff last night."

"Oh, right." I folded my napkin in my lap. "They're great. I've been working on the Christmas Wishes."

Sebastian rubbed his jaw. "It's cool that you're doing that. Maybe I should think of something too. The shop could use a boost in public image." He didn't mention anything that happened last October and neither did I.

The front door opened again, and Jessie came in, her cheeks rosy from the cold. Nancy pulled someone's kid away from her Christmas countdown, which was a large Santa cut-out with a bag over his shoulder that had the number four, then walked over to her.

Jessie said something, and Nancy's eyes widened. The metal silverware slipped from her hand and clattered to the wooden floor.

What had Jessie said to cause *that* reaction?

I rose to help Nancy clean up the mess and find out what was going on, and bumped into someone behind me. "Sorry," I mumbled without taking my gaze from my friends.

"Harp?"

I froze, the air rushing from my lungs. I knew that voice. It was a voice I hadn't heard in almost a year and one I'd never planned on hearing again.

Slowly, I tilted my head back to look up at the person I'd collided with.

Tate the Lying Cheater.

Chapter 3

The Accidental Boyfriend

"Tate?" My voice came out a whisper. "What are you doing here?"

His appearance brought a rush of memories to the surface. Tate proposing with the One Ring and the feel of the cool, smooth metal on my finger. Tate and I snuggled on the couch with a fuzzy blanket, reading *The Legend of Sleepy Hollow*. Him bringing me breakfast in bed when I was sick and the sweet taste of the peppermint tea he would make me. And then Tate and Ashley in bed together.

"I wanted to see you." He took my hand in his large, familiar one. He even had the same callus on the side of his pointer finger from all the writing he did at work.

I gaped up at him. This couldn't be real. Tate couldn't be here in Whisper Hollow. This was my safe place—my place that wasn't contaminated by memories of him. "But why?"

"I wanted to see how you're doing." He smiled, his lips forming an inviting curve that highlighted his strong jaw and the smattering of freckles on his cheeks. They added a touch of youthful innocence to his face that had lured me in last time. But I knew better now.

Suddenly, I was acutely aware of Sebastian next to me. I'd told him all about Tate one day—obviously, I'd never expected the two of them to meet. If only I could turn to study Sebastian and decipher what the lines on his brow meant or the glimmer in his eyes. Things were so much clearer in books.

"Harp?"

Tate's voice snapped me back to this moment—to the very real and odd predicament of having my ex-fiancé standing in front of me while I was on a date—no, not a date—with another guy.

I jerked my hand free from his and scrambled to my feet. My chair scraped against the floor at my sudden rise. "Tate, this is Sebastian. Sebastian, Tate." I quickly introduced them, then grabbed Tate's sleeve and dragged him toward the door. "Sorry Sebastian, but Tate and I need to talk. Outside."

As we passed each table, I could feel the onlookers' curious stares, but I resisted the urge to glance back and meet Jessie's or Nancy's gaze. Or worse, Sebastian's.

A gust of wind slapped me in the face as we stepped outside, helping to ground me firmly in whatever strange reality I was in right now.

"I don't understand. Why are you here?" I let go of Tate and took a step back, placing the building at my back for support. Then I crossed my arms across my chest to keep him from going for my hand again.

He tugged his Christmas beanie—one *I* had given him years ago—lower over his ears. "I regret how things ended, and I had to see for myself that you're okay."

The cheerful carolers working their way down Main were at odds with the shock flowing through me. Tate's appearance was like throwing a bomb on a house and blowing it to pieces.

Tate stepped nearer, and his broad form partially blocked the wind. "Please hear me out. I need to talk to you."

"The time for talking is done." Annoying tears burned at my eyes, and I prayed they'd go away. They were tears of anger, not heartbreak. I was well over Tate. Hopefully, he would think they were from the biting wind.

"Give me a chance, Harp." He took another step forward. We were far too close. I shouldn't have stopped here—now I was trapped between him and the building.

"In case you forgot, Tate, you ruined your chance." I stared down at his shoes. Even his stupid loafers brought back a memory of when we'd gotten lost on a road trip and gone on a spontaneous hike even though he'd been wearing them. "It's too late."

Next to me, the door opened with a jingle, but I didn't look over to see who it was because then I'd risk meeting Tate's gaze again.

"Come on, Harp, please," he pled. "I'm sorry to spring this on you. I tried to call you last night when I got into town, but you didn't answer."

That was because I'd finally taken Grace's advice and blocked his number.

He licked his lips and continued. "I've been wanting to talk to you, so when you didn't answer, I decided to surprise you."

Another surprise from Tate was not what I needed. The memory of his last surprise sent a sick feeling rolling through me. "How many times do I have to tell you to leave me alone?"

"I know, but I really want to talk to you."

I scoffed. Typical Tate. Only thinking about what he wanted. What else could I do to get it through his thick head that we were permanently over?

"She didn't answer because she was with me last night," a deep baritone said from my left.

My head whipped up, and I met Sebastian's gaze. We were definitely not together last night, since we'd both gone home alone after Helen's intrusion, but Sebastian's interference was like an answer to a prayer.

Sebastian lowered his chin in the barest hint of an acknowledgment, as if we had some sort of secret we shared.

Tate straightened and turned from me slightly. "Who are you?" He narrowed his brown eyes and took one step in front of me. But it didn't make sense. Why would Tate be jealous when he'd been the one to cheat on me?

"Sebastian Moore." He moved closer to me.

From the moment Tate had walked through the door of Sugarplum Delights, it was as though I'd stepped into some sort of weird Dr. Who alternate dimension. Even though I was surrounded by normal, familiar things, everything was strange and nonsensical.

Another gust of wind crept under my coat and wrapped around me like an icy hug, reminding me that no matter how strange this was, it *was* real.

"Why was she with you last night?" Tate asked. The stupid guy was so worked up with testosterone that he didn't even ask me.

Sebastian raised one eyebrow in his signature move and stepped past Tate, forcing him back. "You think someone like Harper would stay single and wait around for you?"

My stomach took off in butterflies at his words—maybe butterflies was too calm a word. It was more like a rocket lifted off in my stomach. When Sebastian reached over and wrapped an arm around me, the sensation only grew more intense.

"Harper and I are together now," he said, "and I'd appreciate it if you'd leave my girlfriend alone."

I gaped at Sebastian, trying to remind myself to keep breathing.

"Your girlfriend?" Tate's eyes widened, and his gaze flicked between us with shock and something like disappointment.

"Yes." Sebastian pulled me to his side, pressing me against his warm, solid body.

That's when I remembered to close my mouth.

Tate turned to me. "Harp, are you seriously dating this guy? He's all wrong for you."

I bristled. "I—"

The door opened next to us and Nancy poked her head out, releasing the scent of warm cocoa and coffee onto the street. "Everything okay out here, Harper?" Her face was still pale from whatever Jessie had told her earlier, but her laser focus narrowed in on Tate, then on Sebastian's arm around me.

"Yes," I hurried to assure her before she said anything else. I wasn't sure what was worse at this point—her misunderstanding about Sebastian and me or her undoing Sebastian's lie and giving Tate hope. "We're good. Thanks, Nancy."

"Okay, well hurry inside. You'll freeze out here." She gave me a look that promised we'd talk about it later, and I held back a sigh. Having Nancy around was like having Grace watching over me—great most of the time, except they always found out and read into *everything*.

The door clicked shut behind her, and for a minute we all stood frozen while snow began to drift around us. It was like we were trapped in a snow globe, motionless and frozen in time while we waited for someone to shake things up.

Tate turned back to me. "Harp?" That one word held a world of pleading, but I was through letting Tate affect me.

"You had your chance."

"Can we at least talk?"

I straightened my spine, drawing comfort from the warmth and weight of Sebastian's arm around my waist. "We're done talking."

Tate's head drooped, as if he was only now feeling the guilt from his actions. "I'm sorry."

"Your apology is ten months too late." Though whether it happened then or now didn't matter. Accepting it felt too much like forgiving him.

His gaze met mine, and he started to move, but then stopped and glanced at Sebastian. "I—"

"Sebastian?" A new voice joined the conversation as Helen came to a stop by our group. She took in Sebastian's arm around me and Tate with a curious gaze. "What's going on?"

Sebastian glanced at me almost as if he were apologizing for his lie spreading even more. Little did he know if there was anyone I didn't mind sharing this lie with, after Tate, it was Helen.

Sebastian cleared his throat. "I'm dating Harper."

A hint of betrayal flashed through her gaze. "You didn't say anything about a girlfriend last night."

"I told you I was waiting for someone."

Helen's glare matched the icicles hanging from the roof of Sugarplum Delights overhead. If not for Sebastian's arm around me and the solid wall behind me, I might've taken a step back. Why did she look like she wanted to hurt me? She didn't even know me.

A shiver raced down my spine.

"You should go, Tate," I said, trying to shrug off the uncomfortable atmosphere.

He gave me one last disappointed look, then turned and walked down the street.

"I guess I should go too." Helen walked off with another glance at Sebastian, her heels clinking against the snow-crusted sidewalk.

I watched Tate until he was out of sight, disappearing as quickly as he'd appeared, but the whole time I was hyper-aware that Sebastian hadn't let go of me. The warmth of his hand bleeding through my sweater. The rise and fall of his chest. The way his breath left white puffs in front of us.

"Are you okay?" he said after a moment.

I stood a little too stiffly, unsure if I should move away from Sebastian or not. "Yeah." At least I would be, once the shock wore off.

"I can't imagine what it would be like if my ex showed up like that." His gaze roved over me, filled with concern.

"Thanks for your help." I shook my head. "I can't believe he showed up here with no warning and just expected me to forgive him."

"I get it. Sometimes I still struggle to forgive Coop for what he did and how he left me alone."

This was one reason Sebastian and I had gotten so close the last few months. Our shared trauma of betrayal made it easy to talk.

I sucked in a shaky breath, my gaze falling to his hand that still rested on my hip. "Thank you for stepping in back there."

Sebastian dropped his hand as if remembering he still held me, and the cool air rushed to take its place. "I'm sorry for lying. You were doing a good job on your own, but when he kept ignoring what you were saying, I guess I snapped. I couldn't stand the thought of you with him."

"You couldn't?" I asked breathlessly. His words sent my emotions on a rollercoaster ride.

"No." His gaze met mine, sending a different kind of shiver through me. "I was serious about how amazing you are. That loser isn't good enough for you, and some guy would be lucky to have you." Despite his words, he took a step back, making it clear *he* wasn't the lucky guy.

"Oh, well, thanks. And thanks for your help earlier."

"It's the least I could do," he said. "Your friendship is important to me, and I don't want to mess it up. You're one of the few people in town I can be myself with."

Right. Friendship. The dreaded Friend Zone. That's exactly where we were, and I was grateful for it. It was a miracle we'd even made it there. Hadn't I thought that the other day? So why was it so disappointing to hear him say it now?

The wind howled again, and I shivered.

"You're cold." He reached for the door. "We should go inside."

Going inside and pretending everything was normal after what happened would be way too hard. I needed to process everything. I needed to call Grace.

"I think I'll grab my stuff, then call it a night."

As soon as we stepped inside, Nancy came over. I braced myself for a barrage of questions, but she said, "Have you heard? I found out from Jessie. She's just as bad at keeping secrets as those kids she's always watching."

Which was ironic coming from Nancy, who was the gossip queen of Whisper Hollow.

"Heard what?" When Nancy didn't ask about Tate, the tension in my shoulders relaxed. But as I focused on the worried lines on her face and the way she twisted her apron strings around her finger, my stomach tightened with nerves.

Nancy looked from side to side, where most of her customers still chattered over their dinners, then back at Sebastian and me. "Someone"—her voice wobbled, so she sucked in a breath and whispered—"someone else in town was killed."

Chapter 4

Breaking the Curse

S hock slammed into me again. "What? Who?" I remembered the flash of the lights from the police car speeding down Main this morning, and nausea curled in my gut. Was that where they'd been going?

Sebastian's eyes widened, and he took a step closer to me.

"I'm sure we'll hear soon enough," Nancy said. A customer called her name, and she tucked a strand of gray hair behind her ear with a sigh. "I better go. Be safe out there."

We grabbed our stuff, then walked back into the frigid cold.

"I'll walk you to your car." Sebastian followed me into the alley. "Who do you think it was?" he asked once we were alone again.

"I don't know. It could be anyone." And that thought was almost as terrifying as the knowledge that *another* murderer was on the loose.

First Tate and now a dead body? What else could go wrong tonight?

We fell into silence, and our footsteps filled the spaces in the conversation neither of us seemed capable of.

A meow sounded in the alley, so I cleared my throat and called for Jiji. She often wandered around here at night.

A few seconds later, a thump sounded as Jiji landed on a trash can. She meowed again, her eyes shining in the darkness.

"Come on, girl." I walked over and tried to pick her up, but she leaped from my arms and wound herself around Sebastian's legs.

"Little terror," Sebastian muttered, though his tone was more affectionate than it used to be. He even bent down with a resigned sigh and ran a hand down her back. She arched into his touch with a contented purr.

"Time to go." I tried to pick her up again, but she avoided my hands and prowled toward one of the trash cans, then meowed at the ground. "Seriously, Jiji, stop messing around."

Despite my complaints, she continued her incessant meowing.

"Looks like she found something." Sebastian picked up a wrapper that looked like a piece of trash.

My stomach dropped. It matched the color of what I'd found outside my house that morning, though this scrap was larger, revealing a few letters.

"Oh no," I whispered, staring at it with wide eyes.

"What's wrong?" Sebastian straightened and scanned the alley.

"I've seen that before." My voice shook. "I found something similar this morning, alongside some footprints outside my house."

Sebastian frowned and moved closer. "Are you sure it's the same?"

"Yeah, it has the same design here." I pointed to the small red triangle in the corner. I hadn't recognized it on the other scrap because it'd been cut off, but now I could clearly see it.

"It seems like too much of a coincidence to find the same thing outside your home and your workplace."

"You're right," I said over my pounding heart. "I think someone is following me."

Sebastian's hand curled into a fist, wrinkling the paper. "Considering what Nancy told us, that's less than reassuring."

"I know." My voice came out shaky. Could it have been Tate? It seemed too coincidental that I'd found those footsteps outside my house only to have him show up in town the next day. But if it had been him, why hadn't he tried to talk to me?

"Can I follow you home and make sure everything's good at your house?"

"I'd love that."

He held my door open for me, then got into his car and followed me home. I clutched the steering wheel the entire drive home. I couldn't call Grace yet. Not until I knew what was happening.

I pulled into my driveway, and except for the cheerful glow of my Christmas tree coming through the window, the house was dark and foreboding.

"Thanks again for coming." I unlocked my front door and sucked in a bracing breath of pine from the wreath.

"I'm doing this as much for myself as for you," Sebastian said. "I'll feel better once I know everything is fine."

His words softened the day's chill. Sebastian was so thoughtful. Even though we weren't dating, he still went out of his way to make sure I was okay. Knowing he'd do something like this for someone who was just a friend made him even more attractive.

I pushed the door open, and Sebastian grabbed my arm to keep me from going in first. Nervous butterflies flapped in my stomach, either from his touch or from what he was here to do. Jiji darted between our legs and ran into the house with a meow.

Sebastian walked in and I followed, latching the deadbolt and flipping on the hall light as I went.

"I'm sure everything's fine," I said. But if things were fine, why had I seen those footprints outside my window? Why had I found that same inconspicuous wrapper near Whispering Pages that matched the one outside my house? Finding one was garbage; finding two was a pattern.

Things were most definitely *not* fine.

Sebastian continued into the living room, taking in the Christmas tree and the decorations on the mantle with a cursory glance.

"Outside that window is where I saw the footprints." I pointed to the semicircular window above the sofa and peered through the frosted windowpane, scanning for any sign of movement. Last night's footprints were long gone, and even mine from this morning were partially covered again from today's brief snowfall.

Sebastian clenched his jaw and looked through the glass, then continued his sweep of the house.

Having him there slowed my pounding heart. Or made it speed up for a different reason. It had been a while since I'd had anyone besides Jessie or María over. I followed Sebastian into the kitchen and stood by the counter, running a finger over the poinsettia's soft petals while he did a quick sweep of the room.

"You like decorating for Christmas, don't you?"

Was he genuinely curious or trying to make conversation to break the building tension? I clasped my hands together to resist the urge to reach for him. "You should've seen this place when Nana lived here."

"I did." He flashed a smile at me over his shoulder before heading for the staircase. The glow from my tree highlighted the worry lines on his face. "I guess I should commend you for your restraint. She had a ridiculous amount of decorations."

It was sort of odd thinking of Sebastian being at Nana's house before I even knew him, to think of him having memories of Nana I knew nothing about. "Why don't you like decorating?" It was something I'd noticed back at Halloween. His shop had been one of the few undecorated storefronts on Main.

We made it to the landing, and he searched my room, checking in the closet, behind the door, under the bed, and anywhere else someone could hide. Thank goodness I'd made my bed this morning.

"I don't have the best memories of the holidays." His voice was gruff.

"Why not?" Curiosity battled against the tension running through me like a live wire.

He moved into the guest room without answering, and the floor creaked under his heavy footsteps. "When I was a kid, my dad left our family on Christmas Eve."

"I'm sorry." His heartbreak called to my own, reminding me of Tate's visit and how vulnerable relationships—any relationships—made us.

"It's okay." He shrugged. "To make matters worse, my last girlfriend broke up with me on Christmas, so I haven't had great luck with the holiday. Considering the rocky start to the relationship, I shouldn't have been surprised, but I still was."

"Was she one who played hard to get?" I remembered his comment a while back about how cats tried when you didn't care, but as soon as you showed interest, they played hard to get.

He raised one eyebrow. "I guess I'm not the only one good at remembering things."

I shrugged one shoulder. "It isn't often I hear women compared to cats, you know."

He chuckled, then made his way to the final door—Nana's room. "Yeah, I didn't realize she was playing with me until it was too late, but time heals all wounds, as they say." He pushed the door open, and my bedroom door slammed shut behind me.

I screamed.

"It's okay." Sebastian squeezed my hand. "That happens a lot in old houses. It was probably just a draft, but I'll check the room again after this."

"Sorry." I flushed as I realized I'd reached for him in a moment of weakness. I let go and moved to the doorway to pet Jiji while he checked Nana's room.

"This is my first Christmas without Coop." His low voice came from the darkness of the room.

"I'm sorry."

"I've never been alone before." He stepped back into the hall and shut the door behind him. "At least not like this."

"You aren't alone." The words were out before I could think twice.

His gaze met mine, and the air sparked between us.

Sebastian cleared his throat. "Looks like everything's clear, but I'll check the door that slammed once more to be safe"

"Thanks for doing that." I let go of his hand and fiddled with the edge of my sweater as I followed him to the front door.

"Are you going to be okay here alone?"

"I'll be fine."

"I still think you should mention this to the sheriff." He clenched his jaw. It was hard to tell if it was the idea of the sheriff or of me being in danger that caused that reaction.

"If something else happens, maybe I will," I said. "Right now, it seems like jumping the gun since we don't even know anything yet. Maybe I'm blowing things out of proportion."

He gave me a hard look, and the furrow on his brow communicated his disapproval. But all he did was sigh and say, "Okay, if you need anything, call." He opened the door, and a blast of chilly air swept down the hall.

"I will." I shivered and wrapped my arms around myself. "Thanks again for driving out here to check on things."

"Anytime." He closed the door.

I locked it behind him and stared at the smooth wood for a long moment, then jumped when Jiji twined around my ankles.

"You have got to stop doing that." I scooped her up before settling on the couch and calling Grace.

True to form, she picked up almost immediately. "So did you talk to Sebast—"

"Tate's here," I blurted out before she even finished. There was so much more to tell her, but at least this wouldn't freak her out and make her threaten to fly out here again.

"What?" A string of expletives followed the screech.

I yanked the phone away from my ear until her voice dropped to a lower decibel.

"What's he doing there? Why did he come? What did he say?"

"He said he's sorry, and he wants another chance."

More swearing on Grace's end, and that time I made out one of the kids saying something about the swear jar. "Did you tell him to take a hike?"

"I tried, but he didn't listen, and then Sebastian told him we were dating."

"You and Sebastian?" she screeched. "Tell. Me. Everything."

While I filled her in, I stroked Jiji, who was shedding tiny black hairs all over my soft cream throw. Even with the lights on, the Christmas tree's multicolored lights reflected off the glass decorations around the room.

"Wait, so let me get this straight: Sebastian called you his girlfriend?"

"Yes, but only because he was doing me a favor."

"Which he was," Grace said. "Obviously, you can't give Tate the Lying Cheater another chance."

"Have a little faith in me." I resisted the urge to pull my knees up to my chest and wrap my arms around them, since it would disturb Jiji. "I wouldn't do that."

"Maybe I would if you'd persuade me you're over him."

"I *am* over him."

"I said persuade me, not tell me." She paused, then added, "Like by dating someone else."

"There is no one else." I hurried to add, "I mean, not in *that* way. Just that there's no one to date." My thoughts flashed to a pair of bright blue eyes and a teasing dimple.

"Doesn't Sebastian count?" she said, as if she were reading my mind.

"That wasn't real, Grace," I reminded her. "Besides, he went out of his way to remind me today of how much he values my friendship."

"You never know. Maybe it could be. Getting hurt once doesn't mean you give up forever. Love is about putting yourself out there until you find someone worth getting hurt for."

Jiji meowed at me, letting me know my hand had stopped moving and she didn't approve.

"Like you said, it wasn't once." I resumed petting her. "It was five times." My string of boyfriends before Tate wasn't very impressive.

"Well, maybe Sebastian will help you break the curse."

"I hardly think a fake relationship counts as breaking the curse," I said. "Also, it was a one-time thing. We aren't dating or fake-dating. Sebastian did that while Tate was around, and since Tate is leaving, there's no need for us to pretend anymore."

"Who's the one pretending here, Harp?"

I didn't have a good answer to that.

Chapter 5

Ghosts of Christmas Past

The next morning, Jiji jumped on my chest and jolted me awake. Swallowing a curse, I pet her silky back and glanced out the window. Ice coated each needle of the pine trees and dead grass, refracting the rising sun and turning the world into a sparkling wonderland.

I fed Jiji breakfast, then went for a quick run, my breath puffing in front of me in white bursts. One quick shower and an even quicker breakfast later, I headed to my car, ignoring Jiji's meows for more attention. She was such a drama queen in the morning.

The biting air caused my exposed skin to tingle, but I sucked in an invigorating breath and headed to the car. The crunch of my footsteps on the frozen ground broke the hushed silence. With the sunlight streaming across everything, my fears from last night seemed ridiculous and unfounded, and the news about the murder unreal. I couldn't believe I'd had Sebastian come and check out my house because I'd found some garbage and a couple of footprints.

Wary of the ice on the roads, I let Jiji jump into the car with me and carefully drove to work. After parking behind the shop, I hurried into Nancy's for a hot chocolate to start my day. The tantalizing scent of baked goods and the happy chatter of customers greeted me as soon as I opened the door. The countdown on Santa's bag now said Christmas was only three days away.

"I thought you'd be back again today," Nancy called as I approached the register. A garland made from pine, holly, and red velvet bows stretched across the counter, framing a selection of gingerbread cookies shaped like snowmen and reindeer. Mince pies dusted with powdered sugar sat next to artfully decorated fruitcakes.

"Considering you won't tell me the special ingredient in your cocoa, that's a pretty safe bet."

"If I did, how would I get you to come over and tell me the news?" She passed me a steaming cup and one of her famous cinnamon rolls.

"That's exactly what I was thinking," I said. "Any updates?"

"Still nothing." She shook her head while she decorated a few reindeer cookies. As the town's gossip queen, the lack of news was eating at her. "And what about you? What was Tate doing here?"

I jerked at her casual mention of my ex, and a few drops of steaming liquid splattered onto my finger. I swore and wiped it off. "How did you know that was Tate? Actually, how do you even know about Tate?" In my attempts to move on after settling here, I'd never said anything to her.

Nancy gave me an incredulous look. "You think Bettye hadn't told me all about Tate?"

"But I didn't—"

"Just because you weren't visiting as much didn't mean Bettye wasn't keeping up with your life. Besides, who else could it have been with the way you rushed him out of here? You should have seen the way Sebastian was staring after the two of you." She brushed her hands against her apron, then leaned against the counter. "So?"

I took a tiny sip of my steaming drink to stall, even though it scalded my tongue. The whipped cream complimented the rich dark chocolate, making it impossible not to go for a second sip. "So what?"

"Why was he here?" She narrowed her eyes at me, then placed a few cookies in the display. "And don't try to keep anything from me, because from where I stood last night, your life was about as intense as a K-drama."

"Tate came to see me."

"You're too good for him." She rearranged cookies shaped like Christmas ornaments and tsked. "Bettye always said it, and I completely agree."

I couldn't help but laugh. "Relax, Nancy. I told him to get lost," I said. "In fact, he's probably long gone by now."

"Good, because there's another thing Bettye and I always agreed on, and now I'm even more sure of it."

"What is it?" I asked as the bell at the front door jingled.

"Tate isn't the one for you." She straightened and turned to face the approaching customer. "Sebastian is."

I took another sip instead of responding. Nancy was letting her imagination get away with her again. As evidenced by her Korean drama reference, she loved to see romance everywhere, even when there was none. Not that there couldn't be with Sebastian. He was well beyond just-friend material in my mind, but he didn't seem interested in being more than that in reality. Even after we'd started our weekly dinner ritual, he'd done nothing to make me think there could be something between us. Well, aside from how he'd gallantly stepped in as my fake boyfriend last night, but I wouldn't read into that and start overanalyzing everything. Sebastian only wanted to help, and I was grateful for having him in my life in whatever way I could.

I was fine with friendship. I had to be. Even if his fake announcement last night almost caused my heart to burst.

"Hey, Nancy. Can I have my usual?" a woman called as she came up behind me.

"I'll have it right out, Helen." Nancy turned around to make her drink.

I stiffened and whirled around so fast that I almost spilled my drink on the pretty brunette behind me. "Whoa, sorry."

"No stain, no foul." Helen drummed her nails on the counter, her cold gaze taking me in.

I resisted the urge to cover up my old jeans and T-shirt that said, 'I'm not anti-social. I'm pro-book.'

"So, you and Sebastian, huh?" she said.

"Yup." It slipped out before I considered if I should still keep the ruse up or not with Tate gone, but if Sebastian was willing to help me out of an awkward dating situation, the least I could do was repay the favor.

I glanced toward the door. Was it too rude to make my escape without dealing with the chit-chat? Even though Helen and I had never spoken before, something about her set me on edge. Maybe it was her blatantly trying to cheat on her boyfriend with Sebastian, and how that reminded me of Tate.

"I better get to work, Nancy," I called out across the counter before the awkwardness could get too prolonged. "Thanks for the cocoa. It's delicious."

"I'll see you later, hun." Nancy waved and returned her attention to whatever cup of steaming goodness she was making.

"Have a nice day." I hurried past Helen to the door, unable to shake the sensation of her watching my every step. How did Tom date her? It would be like dating a snake—in more ways than one. If he made one wrong move, she'd strike.

Wait, Tom never came back yesterday. Maybe he'd realized what a terrible girlfriend Helen was and decided not to bother with the present.

Juggling my drink and cinnamon roll, I struggled to unlock the front door of the bookshop.

"Can I give you a hand?" The redheaded man from yesterday held a hand toward me. He gave me a small smile, which made him seem closer to my age. "You look like you could use one."

"Oh, sure." I held out my cup. "If you don't mind holding this for a minute, that'd be great."

I finally got the key in the lock. "Thanks for your help."

"No problem." He returned my drink and glanced inside, then scratched his chin, which was covered in a short-cropped beard that matched his coppery hair. "It's a nice little shop you've got here."

"Thanks." I stood there, unsure if he was going to walk by or come in.

"You're Harper, right?" The man shifted his weight to his other foot. With his broad shoulders and flannel shirt, he gave off faint lumberjack vibes. A short lumberjack, but there was muscle hidden underneath his bashfulness.

"Have we met?"

He flushed. "Not yet, but I knew your grandmother."

Of course he did. Apparently, everyone did.

"I'm Loren, by the way."

"Nice to meet you."

He glanced at his watch. "I better get going. Maybe I'll swing by again." It came out more like a question.

"Come back anytime." I flashed him a smile and opened the front door. Jiji darted from around the corner and into the shop, nothing but a flash of black fur and red velvet from the bow I'd tied around her neck. She ran straight to the Christmas tree and batted at some ornaments hanging on the lower branches. For a moment, the tree was the only illumination in the shop, and I admired how it reflected off everything before flipping on the rest of the lights.

"Jiji, stop it," I called over as I ran through the morning chores, like turning off the security system, tidying the front, and turning on some Christmas carols. Thankfully, Nana's selection of Christmas records outnumbered her Halloween selection, so I'd been cycling through different songs in December. Even so, I was in the mood for something more modern, so I connected my phone and played a Christmas playlist from there.

A steady stream of customers came in and out throughout the morning. After a lull during the lunch break, the door opened again. I looked up from the display of Christmas books I was organizing near the front. "Welcome to Whispering—Oh hey, Sebastian."

"Hey." He took another step into the store, and his broad shoulders seemed to fill the entire space.

"What are you doing here?" Belatedly, I tacked on, "So early."

"I wanted to make sure everything was okay last night." He moved so there were only a few feet between us, and Jiji appeared from the shadows to wind around his legs. "I know you were freaked out."

"And here I thought I'd hidden it so well," I said with a slight smile to cover the way my heart skipped a beat. His fake-dating announcement was doing strange things to my ability to breathe normally.

He closed the distance between us. "Maybe you could if you trained yourself to stop biting your nails."

A flush crept up my cheeks. I hadn't thought he'd noticed my bad habit. "I'll work on it."

He gave me a smoldering look, making my heart flutter. "So, was everything okay?"

"Okay?" I scrambled to piece my thoughts together.

"Last night."

Finally, some of the synapses in my brain connected, and I rejoined the conversation. "Oh yeah. It was fine." I forced a laugh. "After this morning, I sort of wonder if I blew it all out of proportion. Someone was probably hiking in the woods and drawn to the light in my house."

He hesitated a moment, and in the sudden silence, the sound of Mariah Carey singing "All I Want for Christmas is You" filled the space between us.

I glanced at my phone regretfully. If only I'd put on something like "Oh, Christmas Tree" or "Hark the Herald Angels Sing." Something safe and decidedly not about romance. Something that didn't suddenly feel like it was belting out my feelings for Sebastian to hear.

But as much as I loved spending time with Sebastian, how could I date him when seeing Tate again last night reminded me exactly how easy it was for people to let you down? If I didn't want to get my heart broken, I had to keep it firmly to myself.

"Harper?" A magnetic look in Sebastian's eyes pulled me toward him.

"Yeah?"

"There's something I need to tell you."

"What is it?" I held my breath as if the quiet inhales and exhales would keep me from hearing whatever Sebastian had to say.

"I've been thinking a lot about last night."

"What about last night?"

"I realized—"

The door jingled as someone else entered, and I spun around in annoyance. As much as I appreciated sales, now was not the time for customers. I stiffened and stared at the man standing by the door. "Tate? What are you still doing here? I thought you left."

Tate stepped into the store, the light from the window temporarily lightening his blond hair like a halo around his head. But he was no angel. Just the man who broke my heart.

Jiji hissed at Tate as he came in. Good. At least we were united in our distaste for bad men.

"I thought about it," he said. "Leaving, I mean."

"So ... why didn't you?" I put my hands on my hips.

"I made that mistake before and I don't want to do it again." Tate approached and stopped next to Sebastian, though he didn't look at him. "I heard what you said last night, but I'm not ready to give up so easily. It's too soon for me to go back to the city."

Next to me, Sebastian stiffened. Clearly, he'd expected his lie to last only a little while, but having Tate stick around put us all in an awkward position. To his credit, he held his tongue, leaving it up to me to choose what to say to Tate.

"That's not necessary." I tried to usher him out the door, but he didn't budge, so all I did was uncomfortably close the distance between us.

"I never stopped loving you," Tate said in a low voice. "If you give me a chance, I know I can win you back."

"You can't win me like I'm some sort of carnival prize." Frustration bubbled up in me like a boiling kettle of tea until I felt ready to scream. "You're better off putting your efforts elsewhere."

"Preferably somewhere other than my girlfriend." Sebastian stepped up to join me and claimed my hand in his large one. His eyes were hard as they stared at Tate, but they softened when they met mine.

My racing pulse slowed a bit as he took his place by me.

"You say you're over me, but I don't believe it." He reached forward as if he were going to touch my face. Sebastian stiffened, and I leaned back, but all he did was grab something off the bookshelf. When he brought his hand back around, he held the glass book he'd given me a few years ago. "If you don't care, why do you still have this?"

I flushed. "Because it's a bookish Christmas decoration, and this is a bookshop."

"Is that the only reason?" His voice was low and husky.

"Yes, that's all. You can have it back if it means so much to you." I held up the hand joined with Sebastian. "Unlike you, I'm not interested in dating more than one person at a time." Despite the fact that I was over Tate, a hint of spite crept into my tone.

He flinched. "Harp, I said I'm sorry."

"That doesn't change what you did," I said, not even bothering to bring up how he'd killed my credit score along with my trust. His money issues were the least of our problems. "Actions speak louder than words. And even if I wanted to, which I don't, you can't have any relationship without trust."

His jaw worked as if he tried to come up with the right words—a quirk I used to find endearing. "I know we can't. That's why I'm here. I'll show you I'm serious. I know I could do better this time. I've changed."

"Can't you take a hint?" Sebastian's tone was a low growl. "She isn't interested in dating you. In fact, it doesn't even sound like she's interested in seeing you again."

"That's for her to decide," Tate said.

"She has decided, but you aren't listening."

The two men glared at each other. While I was grateful for Sebastian's efforts in his role as my fake boyfriend, I also didn't want them to get into a fight.

"You should go, Tate." I met his gaze, letting the warmth from Sebastian's hand steady me.

The door jingled again, and I turned toward it with relief. "Welcome to Whispering Pages where every book has a story to tell."

"I'm afraid I'm not here for a book today." Sheriff Warner ducked his head at me, but his attention quickly shifted to Tate, then Sebastian.

"Then what can I help you with?" Out of all the people who could've come through the door to help the situation, the sheriff sat dead last on the list. Well, maybe Helen and the sheriff right above her.

Sheriff Warner ran a hand through his receding hair, then replaced his campaign hat. "I'm here to talk to Sebastian."

If possible, Sebastian grew even stiffer. Things between him and the sheriff had never gotten better after what happened in October.

"About what?" Sebastian ground out.

The sheriff hooked his thumbs through his belt loops. "About the murder of Tom Stevens."

Chapter 6

Deadly Alibis

I blinked and suddenly could only see my decorative skeleton sprawled across the floor and Mr. James's body partially hidden by my display table. The sickly sweet smell in the air. The sticky feel of the blood-coated floor. The knot of anxiety in my stomach as Sheriff Warner accused me of murder.

It didn't make sense. He was in here two days ago buying that book for Helen, and now he was dead. My heart beat rapidly but cold crept across my body.

"Tom is dead?" I gasped, my throat closing on the words.

Sebastian squeezed my hand, the gentle, but firm touch pulling me back to the present. "I'm sorry to hear about Tom, but what does that have to do with me?"

His voice grounded me. The sheriff wasn't here to talk to *me*; he was here to talk to Sebastian. Even still, my heart continued to pound, and I tightened my hold on Sebastian.

"According to witnesses, you and Tom had an altercation at work two days ago—a few hours before he was killed." For a moment, the words hung heavy in the air, as if someone had painted them there with Tom's blood. "I need to confirm where you were between eight and ten that night, but we can continue this conversation somewhere more private if you'd prefer."

My thoughts whirled. If Tom was killed two nights ago, that meant he died the night he came into the shop, which was sometime between six and seven, since I'd gone straight to meet Sebastian for dinner. I hardly knew Tom, but I could have been one of the last people to see him alive.

"Are you suggesting that I had something to do with it?" Sebastian's icy tone contradicted the warmth of his hand in mine.

"I'm just saying that we need to talk." Officer Warner held up his hands in front of him, but the gesture did little to placate Sebastian, who only grew stiffer.

The sounds of "Santa, Can't You Hear Me" played in the background, the cheerful Christmas song making the discussion about murder even more unbelievable.

Tate looked between the two men, then said almost grudgingly, "It wasn't Sebastian who did it."

I gaped at Tate. A second ago he'd seemed ready to throw a punch at Sebastian, and now he was defending him against a murder charge?

Sheriff Warner turned to Tate. "And who are you?"

"I'm Tate Harris." Tate stuck out his hand. "I'm visiting."

"And were you with Sebastian two nights ago during the time of the murder?" the sheriff asked after shaking his hand.

"Definitely not." Tate shook his head and leaned against a bookshelf, somewhat messing up the lights I'd strung across the shelf. "But Sebastian said he was with Harp that night, and she'd never hurt anyone."

A confusing mix of emotions wrestled for control in my stomach. While I appreciated Tate's complete faith in me, he'd also made things infinitely more complicated. Like Bilbo-lying-about-the-One-Ring complicated. It wasn't fair to blame him though, since he was only repeating what Sebastian told him last night. We'd dug our own graves.

"Is that true?" Sheriff Warner turned to me.

I hesitated. If I said no, I'd be ruining Sebastian's chance at an alibi, since he'd gone home after his time with Helen. I'd also undermine the fake relationship he'd built to help me get rid of Tate. But if I said yes, I'd be lying to the police.

I bit my lip. Even though I wasn't with Sebastian the night of the murder, I knew he wasn't capable of something like that. I also knew what it felt like to be unjustly accused of murder.

Sebastian squeezed my hand, though I couldn't tell if it was a plea to help him or a warning. Actually, knowing Sebastian, he probably didn't want me to do anything that might get me in trouble.

And that thought helped firm my resolve.

"Yes." My voice came out wobbly, so I cleared my throat and said it louder. "Yes, I was with him." Or at least I'd wanted to be. Maybe that sort of counted.

And with that, I tied our fates together.

"I'd be happy to answer any of your questions later with a lawyer present," Sebastian said, the last word coming out like a sigh.

Sheriff Warner gazed at him for a long moment, then tipped his hat. "If I have more questions, I'll be in touch." He walked back out the door, taking some of the tension with him and leaving the rest of us in a weird vacuum that made me want to collapse into a chair and deflate.

"He's insane if he thinks you'd ever get mixed up in something like that," Tate muttered. "These small-town sheriffs have no idea what they're doing."

I bit my lip and refrained from mentioning how I'd been the one accused of murder a few months ago. I also didn't mention how the events from Halloween probably factored into Sheriff Warner coming to speak to Sebastian.

Whatever happened, I needed to get rid of Tate so Sebastian and I could talk. "Listen Tate, I appreciate your help earlier, but it's not going to work between us. Please go home."

"I hear you, Harp. I do. But I can't go back yet." He took my free hand, which was on its way to my mouth so I could chew on my nails. "But I don't want you to stress, so I'll leave for now and I'll come find you at the Christmas Festival."

I flushed, hating that he knew me well enough to remember that, and didn't even bother asking how he knew about the festival. There were posters all over town, and some of them mentioned Whispering Pages as a contributor since María and I were invested in the Christmas Wish program.

Once the door closed behind Tate, I walked over and flipped the sign to Closed, then rested my forehead against the cool glass.

"You shouldn't have done that," Sebastian said in a low voice.

"Done what?"

"Lied for me."

I met his gaze. "You lied for me." Not to mention he'd been the one to give me an alibi when Mr. James died.

He crossed his arms. "That was different. I was helping you with your ex-boyfriend. You lied to the police. If something happens now, you'll be implicated too."

"Nothing is going to happen because you didn't do it."

"I should tell the sheriff the truth. I don't want to drag you into this." Sebastian ran a hand through his already tousled hair.

"Like it or not, we're in this together." I brushed my bangs from my face. "Instead of focusing on what we should have done differently, let's figure out what to do now."

He blew out a breath. "You're right. We need more information."

"Then we better go find it," I said.

"I guess that means we'll have to keep pretending to date until your ex leaves town." The corner of his mouth lifted in a half-grin.

"And until the killer is found" I tried to gauge his reaction, but his blue eyes were inscrutable. Meanwhile, my traitorous heart gave a little thump even though this whole thing was a scam. "Otherwise, our alibis will fall apart."

"What sort of fake boyfriend would I be if I didn't help you avoid terrible exes?" He scanned my face as if waiting for something, then gestured toward the door. "Let's figure out the truth behind Tom's murder."

Someone came in, and I whirled around. "We're closed—oh, María."

I blinked at her, pulling myself from Sebastian's spell to ground myself in the reality of Christmas preparation once more.

"Did you forget about our meeting for the Christmas festival?" She gave me a wicked grin, her dancing gaze darting between Sebastian and me.

I tried not to flush and idly tidied the books on a shelf next to me even though they didn't need it. "It's been a crazy day."

"I bet."

"Why don't we meet at Nancy's in an hour?" Sebastian said. "I've got a few things to take care of at the shop before we go."

"Sounds good."

"Hey, Sebastian." Despite her casual tone, I could feel her gaze burning the side of my face. I needed to talk to her about her bad habit of watching people, mostly me, through the store window.

"Hey." He smiled at María, then turned and gave me one last lingering look that sent shivers down my spine before walking down the street toward Grain and Glass.

"All right, spill," María said as soon as the door closed. "You and Sebastian are dating, aren't you?"

"Sort of? We—"

"I knew it. I knew it. I knew it," she squealed and clapped her hands in time with the words.

"Before you get your hopes too high, let me tell you what happened." I gave her a quick rundown of how Sebastian had pretended to be my boyfriend to scare Tate off since he wasn't listening to me, carefully leaving out any details about our fake relationship being part of Sebastian's alibi.

"I'm so happy!" María clapped her hands together.

Something clattered to the floor near the Christmas tree. I walked over and picked up Jiji, who'd been batting at a small nativity ornament again. "You love that Sebastian is pretending to date me to scare off my ex-fiancé?"

"Aw, he's pretending?" She frowned and tugged on the end of one of her dark curls. "Well, that's okay. If there's anything I've learned from reading books and watching Hallmark movies it's that you and Sebastian will fall in love while you kick Tate to the curb. It's going to be like Kate and Curran."

"Is that the *Kate Cane* series?" I glanced over at the mystery section. Kate Cane books were some of my biggest sellers, but I didn't recall them having fairytale endings.

She clucked. "No, Kate Daniels by Ilona Andrews."

I shook my head. "Stop distracting me. The point is, I'm not trying to fall in love. I'm trying to catch a killer." Again. How many times would I have to do that in a town as small as Whisper Hollow?

"Who says you can't do both?" María gave me a sly wink as she straightened the Santa hat on the snowman's head by the front door.

"Don't be ridiculous."

"You're the one being ridiculous. Despite all your protests, I think you're half in love with him already." She folded her arms across her chest. "You don't stand a chance."

I sighed and resisted pointing out how right she sort of was, because that sort of thinking wouldn't do either of us any favors. "Anyway, once we finish going over these details, I need to meet with Sebastian so we can check on some stuff. Can you—"

"Leave it to me." She nodded. "I'll get everything ready for the event."

"Thanks."

We spent most of the next hour going over details, then María gathered up the supplies. "Good luck with your date. Let me know how it goes."

I rolled my eyes but refrained from telling her that it wasn't a date since she was more stubborn than me. "I'll see you later."

Leaving the shop in María's capable hands, I exited through the back door that led to the small parking lot. Since I still had about ten minutes before meeting Sebastian, I settled into my car and called Grace.

"Hey Harp, what's up?"

"Do you have a minute?"

"Sure. I can chat while I shop."

I spilled the entire story from Tate's reappearance to my ridiculous conversation with María, though I had to talk over Grace's frequent interruptions. "And we're going to meet in a few minutes at Nancy's to see what we can find out."

"Are you kidding me? Someone else died?" Grace's shrill voice cut through the AirPod, then she spoke more softly. "I thought Whisper Hollow was supposed to be safe."

"Me too." I started to chew on my nail, then sat on my hand instead.

"Are you sure you don't want to visit for the holidays? You could move your New Year's trip up a few days." The hum of conversation and the distinct ding of a cash register sounded in the background.

I rested my head against the steering wheel and closed my eyes. "I can't leave now. I need to help Sebastian clear his name."

"Technically, he doesn't *need* your help. He needs you to be his alibi."

"Considering he's the reason I even had an alibi when Mr. James was killed and he's helping me with Tate, I feel like I owe him at least this much."

"And how are the two of you planning on clearing his name?"

"We'll have to figure out who killed Tom." I chewed on my bottom lip. "And I think I know where to start. Tom's girlfriend, Helen."

Grace lowered her voice. "You think she'd kill her boyfriend?"

"I don't know, but there's something off about her."

"More than your jealousy from her date with Sebastian?"

"It wasn't a date," I said. "Besides, I wasn't the only one who thought she was odd. Both Nancy and María commented on it too."

I could practically hear Grace shaking her head. "Yes, but being flirty doesn't make someone a killer."

"What about a few months ago?" I said, bringing up the murder from Halloween.

"That's not fair. Correlation isn't the same as causality," Grace said. "But I guess talking to her is as good a start as any, even though the police probably already have. Relatives and romantic partners are some of the first people consulted in a case." After a moment of background noise, Grace said, "So what are you going to do about the Christmas festival?"

"I'm going to pretend like everything's normal and continue with it. Canceling it wouldn't make sense. Unlike last time, the murder doesn't have anything to do with me or the shop, and I still want to work on the Christmas Wishes."

"And what about Sebastian?"

"I already said we're going to clear his name."

She blew out a breath. "I meant about the fake dating. I don't want to see you get hurt."

"I'll be fine. How can I get hurt when everything is pretend?"

"Famous last words," Grace muttered. "But maybe this is what you need. If you're too scared to give someone a real chance, maybe a fake chance will have to do."

I wasn't scared; I was cautious. There was a huge difference.

"I better go," I said before she could lecture me on my dating life again. "I'm supposed to meet Sebastian in a minute."

"Okay. Call me later."

"You know I will." I disconnected, pulling my coat tighter to brace myself for the frigid air before opening the door and stepping out. I slipped on an icy patch and caught myself on my door.

Glancing down, I swore at the icy ground, then my gaze snagged on a cigarette stub.

It had a stripe around the end that was the same blue color as the scraps of paper I'd found in my yard. Seeing it helped the pieces fall into place as a memory rose to the surface. The three pieces were connected to the same cigarette brand. Maybe even literally.

My stomach dropped. I'd told Sebastian that everything was fine, but maybe I wasn't blowing things out of proportion after all.

Someone was watching me.

Chapter 7

Tangled in Tinsel and Lies

As soon as I walked into Sugarplum Delights, I inhaled the scent of coffee and gingerbread. As Nancy tried to finish up chatting with Mrs. Schoenfield and Evelyn, her whole body shifted my way, ready to dart over as soon as her conversation ended.

I smiled, remembering all the times I'd seen Nancy, Mrs. Schoenfield, Evelyn, and Nana strutting around town in their cardigans and pearls. The four of them had been inseparable when I was a kid. Every time we came to visit, we'd find them getting into some sort of trouble. Listening to their stories was like watching an episode of *The Golden Girls*.

While I waited, I spotted the older man who'd come into the shop yesterday at the same time as the redhead who'd stuck around uncomfortably long while I talked to Sebastian. A bowler hat sat on the table in front of him, and he sipped what looked like a cup of coffee.

"Hi." I walked over and smiled. "I'm Harper from the bookshop next door."

"Oh, hi." His eyes widened. Maybe he wasn't used to strangers approaching him. He probably wasn't a Whisper Hollow native. "I'm Walter."

"Are you visiting someone in town?" I asked.

His bushy eyebrows shot up. "How did you know?"

"There aren't many other reasons people come to Whisper Hollow." I laughed and added, "I saw you come in yesterday and thought I'd check if you found everything you were looking for."

He put his cup down and gave me a small smile. "Yes, I did. Thank you for checking."

Realizing it was terrible manners to ask why he didn't buy whatever he'd been looking for if he had found it, I held my tongue, despite my burning curiosity. If there was something I could do better, I wanted to know. But people didn't always appreciate being asked stuff like that.

Despite my restraint, he must have read my thoughts on my face because he laughed. "I'll come by later to grab it. I ran out of time."

"Oh, great." I gave him a wide smile. "If there's anything else you need at the shop, let me know."

"Thank you."

Nancy appeared at my side and put a slice of pie on Walter's table. "This one is on the house, Walter." She winked at him, then pulled me over to an empty corner while I tried to wrap my mind around the idea of Nancy flirting with someone. "It's about time you got here." She wiped her hands on her apron and gave me a stern look.

"Because ..."

Nancy twisted her apron string around one finger. "I saw Leo go into your shop earlier. He doesn't think you have something to do with Tom's murder, does he? Because I can give his mother a call if I need to."

"It's okay, Nancy." I gave her a small smile, touched by her protective nature when it came to the sheriff. "He was there to talk to Sebastian, not me."

"That would make sense. I heard from Lucy, who heard from Jill, who heard from Susan, that Helen was the one who tipped Leo off about Sebastian's fight with Tom."

I blinked, then shook my head, trying to take in her information chain. So, Helen was the one who had pointed the police at Sebastian?

One of Nancy's eyebrows rose. "And what was Sebastian doing at your shop?"

I fumbled to a stop, realizing I'd made a mistake. Sebastian and I both had. We'd agreed to meet at Nancy's without thinking since this was where we always met, but now we had to decide what to do. If I told Nancy that Sebastian and I were dating, the news would be across town faster than Tom's murder. But if I didn't, Tate could find out that we weren't dating. Maybe telling her was the best way to solidify our story.

"Because Sebastian and I are dating now." The lie felt strange ... but also strangely right.

As if summoned by his name, Sebastian came through the door behind me. "Ready to go?" he said, apparently oblivious to the wide-eyed looks Nancy was giving both of us.

"Um, sure."

"Wait a minute." Nancy gestured between the two of us. "When did this happen? Why is this the first I'm hearing about it? How could you drop this on me so casually when I've been waiting for this for years?"

That last part felt a tad dramatic since I'd only met Sebastian a few months ago, but considering how much she and Nana had talked about us, maybe it was accurate.

Sebastian blinked at her, shook his head once, then gave me a rueful grin. "It happened last night."

"Last night?" Mrs. Schoenfield piped up from one of the other tables, where she sat with Evelyn, another woman from the nursing home. "Well, crap." Mrs. Schoenfield got up and hobbled her way over to us, then slipped Nancy a twenty-dollar bill. "I didn't think it would be until after the New Year."

I gaped at her, then at Nancy, who pocketed the money with a smile. "You should know better than to bet against me by now, Sal." Nancy tapped her nose and winked at me. "I have a nose for these things."

"Wait a second"—I held up a hand, then gestured between them—"are you saying you two bet on if Sebastian and I would get together?"

The tips of Sebastian's ears darkened.

"Not if. When." Nancy smirked. "But that's not important right now. Tell me everything. Is this because of Tate's visit?"

"I guess you could say that." Sebastian reached over and took my hand, while Nancy tracked our every move like a hawk. "It made me realize how much I didn't want her to be with him."

Mrs. Schoenfield sighed and elbowed Evelyn while Nancy said, "This is perfect. Now you two can come to the Christmas Festival."

"We were already going to do that." I tried not to pay too much attention to the way Sebastian's hand dwarfed mine and how protected I felt with him next to me.

"Yes, but I mean you can come together. As a couple."

"Sure, I guess so," I said. "We were planning on going anyway to set up the Christmas Wishes."

"Harp is good at giving back to the community like that." Sebastian placed a kiss on my temple, which widened Nancy's grin and almost gave me cardiac arrest. He wasn't playing fair. Where was the surly, awkward guy I first met? And how could he throw out a nickname so casually like that? Only Grace called me Harp these days.

Well, two could play at that game.

I tugged on his hand. "Come on, my little heartwood. We should get going."

He straightened at the nickname, and I held back a smile. It served him right for that kiss. It wasn't fair for me to be the only one thrown off my game.

We left Mrs. Schoenfield and Nancy behind, and as soon as we were out on the street, he turned to me with a little half-smirk that hinted at his left dimple. "Heartwood?"

"What?" I shrugged but couldn't help but notice that he hadn't let go of my hand. "You called me Harp, so it was only fair." It was odd hearing Grace's nickname for me coming from Sebastian, but it was also nice.

"Yes, but heartwood?"

"You love wood. It seemed like a great nickname."

He laughed, a genuine sound that brought a smile to my face. "You should call me Seb. I'm not sure that I trust your taste in nicknames."

"My taste in nicknames is fine, thank you."

"Now you sound like Coop." At his mention of his little brother, his smile fell.

We walked down Main Street in silence. Tinsel-wrapped street-lamps lined each side of the street, looking like they were playing dress up in silver feather boas.

After a moment, Sebastian—Seb—cleared his throat. "So, where should we start?"

A gloom settled over me as I remembered how we were going to try to find out more about Tom's murder. "I was thinking we should go talk to Helen. She's the one who told the police about your fight with Tom."

Seb stiffened. "I guess we should then. I can't see any motive for her, but it's as good a place as any."

"Do you know where she lives?"

"Just that she lives alone."

I couldn't help but be a little relieved. Clearly, he'd never been to her house.

"But I know where she works, so we can start there." Seb led the way down the street.

"Great." I stared at the sidewalk and shoved my free hand into my pocket. The wrapper from the other night crinkled, reminding me of what I'd found outside my car. "Also, I was wrong."

"Nice of you to admit it." Seb flashed me a smile. "But about what specifically?"

I pulled the paper out. "I thought maybe I was overreacting about the footprints outside my house and the wrapper I found, but today I found a cigarette outside my car while it was parked behind the store."

"A cigarette?" His brow furrowed.

"Yeah." I swallowed. "It's a brand with a blue stripe on the box."

Seb's grip on my hand tightened, though the pressure was far from painful. "Considering we found out a murderer is loose in town, I can't say I like the thought of that."

"Me either." I sighed.

"Can I have that wrapper you found?"

"This?" I pulled the scrap of paper from my pocket and handed it to him. "Sure."

"Thanks." He pulled me to a stop and caught my eye. "Harp?"

"Yeah?" My heart pounded at the way my nickname fell from his lips, as if it was something he'd been saying his whole life.

"Can I stay at your place tonight?"

"What?" My heart pounded so loudly, I wasn't sure I'd heard him correctly.

"I hate the idea of you being there alone when this person, whoever they are, knows where you live and work," he said.

I grimaced at the thought. "I do too."

"I can sleep on the couch or whatever, but I'd feel better if I was there."

"You move pretty fast for a fake boyfriend," I teased, trying to hide how his words somehow put me at ease and also made me feel like someone had dropped a bath bomb in my stomach. But there wasn't any way to hide how sweaty my hand felt in his.

"So, is that a yes?"

"I guess so." I might not be able to sleep knowing Seb was in the other room, but that was better than not being able to sleep out of terror. "Thanks for taking care of me again."

He flashed his one-dimple smile at me and tugged on my hand. We moved down Main Street, I assumed in the direction Helen worked. Evergreen garlands with bright red ribbons hung from some store-fronts.

"I don't understand why this is happening," I said after a minute of walking in comfortable silence. "Why would someone be following me?"

"Do you think it's related to Tom's murder? The timing is pretty strange otherwise."

"I don't know why it would be." I resisted the urge to bite my nails. "I only met Tom once, and I have no idea who killed him or what it could have to do with me."

Seb was silent for a long moment, then he shot me a sideways glance. "Do you think this has anything to do with Tate?"

I laughed. "Why do you say that?"

"His timing was also pretty strange. As soon as he showed up in town, all these things started happening."

"True." I chewed on my lower lip. "And now that you mention it, Tate used to smoke, but he quit not long after we started dating. I don't think that was his brand, and he hasn't smelled like cigarettes either time I've seen him."

"He could've started again."

"I know, but I don't think it was him. He's a jerk and a liar, but not a murderer." But if it was him following me, that was less alarming than the alternative.

Seb stayed silent as we passed a family walking by, their arms were loaded with bags and shiny, wrapped packages. Laughter and chatter filled the air, at odds with the tension flowing through me.

"Where does Helen work?" I asked.

"Main Street Makers." With his free hand, he pointed ahead to where the craft store sat not too far away. "Have you ever been?"

"I've only passed by. I've never gone inside." Unlike Nana, I wasn't the crafty type.

The area in front of the shop resembled some winter storybook, with a few animatronic elves and reindeer taking up part of the sidewalk.

"Wow. Did they overdo it much?" I mumbled.

Seb smirked. "I thought you liked decorating for holidays."

"Seems like they're trying too hard. They're a crafts store, not a decorating store."

"Right." Seb squeezed my hand. "When we go inside, maybe let me do the talking. If Helen is here, I'm sure she's shaken up about what happened, and she might be more willing to talk to me."

"Fair enough." I pushed open the front door without stopping to admire the tiny miniature village dusted with artificial snow in the window. It put my tiny Christmas village to shame. Vibrant displays of ribbons, wrapping paper, sparkling tinsel, and ornaments in varying shades of red, green, gold, and silver greeted us as soon as we walked inside. The shop was small and compact, like most of the buildings on Main, and it felt even smaller with the aisles crammed with glass baubles, paint-it-yourself snowflakes, tubes of glitter, and other DIY Christmas projects.

"Sebastian, you came." Helen walked over and her chestnut hair, which hung in loose waves down her back, shimmered with red highlights as she passed through the light from the window. Her wide smile faltered as she noticed Seb holding my hand, and she fiddled with the long necklace that complimented her Christmas earrings and casual red shirt.

"We wanted to check on you," Seb said. "We heard about Tom."

"It was all so sudden." Her lower lip wobbled, and she swiped at her eyes, which were red and puffy. A surge of sympathy flowed through me, but then I reminded myself not to feel too sorry for her yet, since we had no idea what was an act and what was the truth. I'd learned that I wasn't the best judge of character, and Helen had given me strange vibes from the start. After all, how sad could she be when she'd been trying to cheat on Tom with Seb the other night?

"I'm sorry," I said, my words drawing her attention to me.

"You two are still together." She said it like a statement, with a hint of disappointment dripping through her tone, but the eager glint in her eye also made it sound like a question.

"Yes, we are," I said.

Seb let go of my hand and wrapped his arm around my shoulders, and only then did I realize how stiffly I was standing. "How were things between you two?"

"They'd gotten better after that fight we had. It's hard to believe he's gone, ya know?"

"Yeah," Seb murmured, while I tried not to ask her why she was chasing after Seb if things were so good with her and Tom.

"Like he was here one day and gone the next, and I'll never get to see him again." She grabbed a tissue from behind the front desk and dabbed at her eyes again, though considering she'd been ready to hit on Seb a moment ago I didn't believe it as much as before. "I didn't even have a chance to say goodbye."

"Did you notice anything strange the last time you saw him?" Seb asked.

"He seemed a little distracted, but other than that everything was fine," she said. "Well, I mean he'd been acting a little odd lately, but besides that everything was fine."

"Odd how?" I asked.

"I don't know. Just odd. Jumpier than usual."

I probably would be jumpy too if I was dating Helen. I imagined it felt like walking on eggshells.

She shrugged and dabbed at her eyes. "We were supposed to meet up the day he died, but he didn't answer his phone."

"The night at the bakery?" Seb clarified.

She blinked rapidly. "Yeah."

According to Seb, he hadn't stuck around with Helen long, which meant she'd probably tried to call Tom sometime between seven and eight. That time frame matched the window Sheriff Warner had given us.

"After you so rudely left me in the diner"—she sniffed and glared at him—"and Tom didn't pick up, I went home. What else was I supposed to do?"

"So, you were alone." The words slipped out before I realized I'd said them.

Helen stiffened and took one step back. "What are you implying?"

"She wasn't implying anything." Seb shot me a look.

"You sound like the police, asking me all these questions about it, almost as if they thought *I* had something to do with his death. Can you believe it?"

Yes. I thought back to María's words—something about a lioness hunting its prey.

"I'm sorry you had to go through that," Seb said. "The sheriff came and talked to me too, so I know how you feel."

I shot him an admiring glance for the masterful way he brought that up.

Helen glanced away, then back at Seb, the flush on her cheeks darkening. "I'm sorry. That was my fault. They asked if I'd noticed anything unusual with Tom that day, and since he didn't normally have trouble at work, I thought I'd point it out."

"Thanks for telling me." Seb gave her a gentle smile that was at odds with the accusations trying to climb up my throat. Didn't she know it was her fault Tom had been upset? "Can you think of anything else you said to the police?" he asked.

"I reminded them they needed to talk to that guy whose mom died at the nursing home. He never forgave Tom for it, even though it totally wasn't his fault." She shook her head and pushed a lock of her long, auburn hair behind her ear. "I could see him owning a gun though. He seems like the type."

"A gun?" Seb asked. "Is that how Tom died?"

Her brow furrowed. "Yeah. Didn't you know? He was shot, but the gun hasn't been found yet."

"How did the killer get inside his house?" I asked.

She narrowed her eyes at me as if remembering I was there. "I never said he was killed at home. His body was found near the retirement center."

I filed that information away for later.

"Thanks for taking the time to talk to us, Helen. Let us know if you need anything." Seb turned toward the door.

"Sebastian, wait." She put a hand on his arm. "That night after you left ..."

"Yeah?" he said.

She took a deep breath. "I saw someone as I walked home."

"Saw who?" I barely kept my foot from tapping.

"Someone in the alley," she whispered. "I don't know who, but it looked like a man."

I froze. Maybe I hadn't imagined that feeling of unease as I'd gone through the alley. "What did he look like?"

"I don't know. He was hidden in the shadows, but I could tell one thing for sure."

"What?" Seb asked.

"He was smoking."

I shivered. If my stalker *was* related to Tom's murder, how close had I come to the killer?

Chapter 8

Making a List and Checking it Twice

Once we headed back down Main Street, Seb turned to me, his blue eyes full of worry. "That person Helen saw in the alley was probably the one who left that wrapper."

"You might be right, but we still don't know why or if it's related to Tom's murder. None of this makes sense." I chewed on my nail and glanced around the darkening street as night fell across Whisper Hollow. That person in the alley didn't explain Helen's strange behavior, or why she'd been so quick to throw Seb under the bus to the police. I wasn't ready to cross her off the list yet. And then there was the guy from the nursing home.

"It'll be okay. We'll figure it out." Seb took my hand and gave it a reassuring squeeze. "I need to run home and grab a few things before we go to your place."

"Okay." As his words sank in, my stomach fizzed again. Seb was coming over. And not for a few minutes to wash out his pepper-sprayed eyes or to check my house for intruders. He was staying the night.

"I'll meet you at my place." The words rushed out as I thought of the cleaning up I needed to do.

He gave me a worried look as we made it to our cars parked in the small lot behind our shops. "If you're sure."

"I am." I needed a head start.

He watched me get into my car and pull out of the lot.

My fingers shook with nerves as I called Grace. I didn't want to worry her about the person who may or may not be following me, but I could at least get her opinion on having Seb stay over.

She picked up after a few rings. "Hey Harp, what's up?"

"Seb is staying the night at my place. What do I do?" The words rushed out.

"Whoa. Slow down. He's staying the night? I thought this was a fake relationship."

"It is." I blew out a breath and tightened my grip on the steering wheel as I sped through a yellow light and drove past a street of houses dripping with Christmas lights.

"So why is he coming over?"

I spent the few minutes of my drive rehashing what he'd said about not wanting me to be alone because of the murder, while trying to leave out the part about the potential stalking.

"Let me get this straight," she said as I made it home, where my Christmas tree's cheerful glow greeted me through the living room curtains. "Seb's so worried about the murder of someone who has nothing to do with you that he's staying over at your house?"

"Stop smiling." For a moment, I admired how the Christmas lights outlining the roof and wooden porch cast a magical glow on the fresh snow. Everything looked so cozy and safe...deceptively so.

"I'm not," she said. "But even if Sebastian is pretending, he might be the best boyfriend you've ever had."

And the only one whose relationship came with a time limit.

The thought made my heart wrench.

"Oh, shut up." I got out of my car to cover up my momentary silence, and the cold air blasted into me. As I walked to my front door, a bush rustled next to my house and my heart took off. I froze with my key in the lock. My breathing stuttered. Maybe telling Seb I'd meet him here had been a stupid idea.

"Harp, you okay?" Grace said.

"I think there's something—" Jiji darted out of the shadows next to the house and I screamed.

"Harper! What's wrong?"

Jiji wrapped around my legs, and I let out a shaky laugh. "I'm sorry. Jiji came out of nowhere and scared the crap out of me."

Grace swore. "Don't scare me like that."

Once my legs were no longer jelly, I opened my door and Jiji slipped in ahead of me. I closed the door and locked it, then double-checked that I locked it.

"Since when are you so jumpy?" Grace asked.

I sighed. "I think small towns are bad for my heart."

"Or is it the thought of Sebastian coming over that has you so shaken up?"

Her teasing reminded me that he was coming. I rushed to the living room and straightened the plush red blankets and green cushions strewn across the furniture. My gaze swept over the Christmas tree with its shimmering tinsel and twinkling lights, then to the garlands of holly and Christmas village adorning the fireplace mantle. Would Seb like it?

Not that it mattered. He'd already seen it. I was overthinking things.

"I'm not nervous ... I just haven't had anyone stay over for a while." Once I'd reassured myself the rest of the room was fine, I hurried to the kitchen. The table was clear except for the decorative centerpiece made of pine branches, red berries, and golden pinecones flanked by two tall candlesticks, but I took a moment to shove the dishes from this morning into the dishwasher, then dry my hands on one of the Christmas towels hanging from the oven.

"Right." Grace's silences were always louder than her words. "Be careful, Harp."

"Be careful about what?" Did Grace find out something about the stalker after all? I pulled open the fridge, searching for something I could feed Seb when he came over, but the only thing I had that would work was a roll of pre-made sugar cookie dough. Hopefully, Seb liked sugar cookies. What was I saying? Who didn't like sugar cookies?

"About confusing fiction with reality. I don't want to see you get hurt because you can't tell what's real and what's fake."

"You're stressing too much, Grace. I won't get hurt." I set the temperature and tossed the cookies in to bake. As a final thought, I turned on some Christmas music on the speakers. Seb and I didn't usually have awkward silences, but there wasn't anything usual about this situation. "After all, there won't be anything confusing about it since I know it's fake."

"You say that now..."

I made my way upstairs. "Stop worrying and fill me in on the family. How is everyone over there? I feel like I'm always talking about myself when we talk." While I listened to Grace's stories, I closed the door to Nana's room and mine. No way was he getting in there. I went to the guest room and started prepping it. Seb said he'd be fine sleeping on the couch, but that seemed silly when there were extra rooms upstairs. My hands shook as I placed an extra blanket on the foot of the bed. The bed that Seb would sleep in tonight.

Seb was staying the night.

The thought hit me again, and I sucked in a breath, trying to calm down. The scent of fresh cookies drifted through the house and curled around me like a warm blanket.

A knock sounded on the front door.

"He's here. I'd better go." I headed down the stairs as Jiji streaked past me.

"Okay, well don't do anything I wouldn't do," Grace said in her 'I'm half-teasing, half-serious' tone.

"That leaves things pretty open, doesn't it?"

She laughed. "See ya later."

"Bye." I stopped on the other side of the front door and tried to slow my pounding heart. I wasn't sure what was more pathetic. The thought that it was beating so hard from climbing the stairs or from the thought of seeing Seb even though I'd been with him half an hour ago.

Jiji paced in front of the door and meowed once as if scolding me for taking so long.

Sucking in one more deep breath, I pulled open the door.

Seb held a small overnight bag, looking far better than anyone had a right to. His brows, a shade darker than his hair, arched into his hairline and added an intensity to his piercing blue gaze that was only slightly offset by his teasing smirk. "Aren't you going to invite me in?"

"Oh, right. Of course." I held the door open wider, trying not to think too hard about the fact that it looked like he'd fixed his hair. "Come on in."

"Thanks."

As soon as Seb walked through the door, a wave of musk and peppermint hit me, along with a faint hint of salt and grease from the brown bag in his hand. Jiji wrapped around his legs like a black blanket and let out a contented purr. Such a traitor.

He sniffed and looked around. "Wow. Something smells good."

"So do you," I blurted out.

His grin widened, brightening his blue eyes and revealing that darn dimple. It did funny things to my stomach.

"I mean, you smell good because of whatever's in the bag." Realizing I wasn't making things any better, I added, "I thought I'd throw in some cookies in case you were hungry."

"Is that your idea of dinner?" he teased. "Because I thought we could have some burgers and fries while we figured out what to do next."

"That sounds great." I ran to the kitchen to hide my burning cheeks, calling over my shoulder, "I'll get some allergy meds for you."

"You remembered I was allergic to Jiji?" He followed me into the suddenly-too-small room and raised an eyebrow as I dropped a pill into his hand. "Guess I didn't need to bring my own."

"Better safe than sorry. Allergies are the worst." I tried to keep my tone casual. To make sure he couldn't tell how flustered I was, I went to retrieve the cookies before they could burn.

I showed Seb the guest room so he could put his stuff down, then we settled in at the table. I could almost pretend that it was another night eating dinner at Sugarplum Delights if not for the fact that we were alone. While it would've been nice to forget about the murder and the strange happenings around town, with Seb sitting across from me at *my* dinner table eating burgers and pretending to be my fake boyfriend, it was impossible to ignore the reindeer in the room. And considering how suspiciously Helen had acted today, she was surely hiding something. We needed to figure out how to get her to spill the beans.

"What did you think about Helen today?" I asked after a few bites of my burger.

Seb finished chewing, then said, "I'm not sure that it was her."

"What?" I stopped with a fry halfway to my mouth. "Didn't you notice how suspicious she was acting? Plus, she threw you under the bus to save herself. And don't even get me started on the night she was supposed to meet up with Tom, she *coincidentally*"—I raised my fingers in air quotes—"couldn't get ahold of him, and then he shows up dead?"

"But why would she tell us about her lack of an alibi if she killed him? I mean, what reason would she have to kill him, anyway?"

"I don't know. Maybe they got into a fight since she was cheating on him. Maybe Tom owed her money or something. Maybe Tom was cheating on her too and she found out." That one made the most sense. Cheating seemed pretty normal in relationships these days, and I remembered how betrayed I'd felt when I'd found out about Tate and my old roommate.

"I guess it could be her, but it feels like you're overlooking a much more obvious suspect." Seb's blue eyes stared at me as if searching for a way into my soul.

"I am?" I put my fry down. "Who?"

"Tate."

I barely held back a laugh. "You think Tate killed Tom? Talk about a lack of motive. He doesn't even know him."

"Yes, but if you want to talk about coincidences, let's talk about how the night Tate came to town is the same night Tom was killed, and also the same time you started finding evidence of someone following you."

"Technically, we don't know when Tate got to town," I said.

"Yeah, but you said it yourself that he used to smoke."

"Exactly. *Used* to," I said, wishing I could remember the brand he used to smoke to further prove my point. "Tate has no reason to stalk me. Not when he's already come up to talk to me twice on his own."

"Why are you so quick to defend him?" Seb clenched his jaw.

"Why are you so quick to dismiss Helen as a possibility?"

A tense silence settled between us at the table, broken only by the soft sounds of "Silent Night" playing in the background.

"Well, I guess we'll need to keep looking into both of them as possibilities," I said.

"I'm sorry. I didn't mean to get worked up. I'm just worried and I can't believe he thinks he deserves another chance after hurting you." Seb sighed and reached across the table to take my hand.

I started at the contact. There wasn't anyone around, but he was still being so gentle. "It's okay. It felt like when we first met and argued all the time." I offered a small smile as a peace offering.

"Maybe so." He returned it, then squeezed my hand. "But I don't want to fight anymore. I think we're past that now."

"I'm sorry too," I offered. "Clearly I need to work on the whole fake girlfriend thing."

Seb withdrew his hand and nodded. "Yes, I guess we both do. Well, obviously I'm not your girlfriend. I was referring to the dating part. Or the fake dating part. But if it makes it more believable, I'd be more than happy to punch Tate the next time he looks at you."

I laughed. "I appreciate the offer, but I prefer it when you use your hands for other things."

He raised an eyebrow, and my cheeks heated again as I replayed my words in my mind. Why did I always say things the worst possible way when Seb was around?

"I was talking about for work and stuff." There were few things more attractive than Seb talking about his passion for woodworking.

He ran a hand through his tousled hair, trying—but failing—to hide his grin. "I see."

"Anyway, I was thinking about the Christmas Festival tomorrow. I think we should go."

"I agree," he said, thankfully changing subjects with me. "Helen told me she was planning on going—or at least she said that before everything happened with Tom—and the other day, Tate also mentioned he was going. It's the perfect chance for us to talk to them again."

With Christmas three days away, it would be nice to wrap things up before the holidays. It was hard to feel like Christmas with a murderer on the loose. But at the same time, my stomach gave a twinge of disappointment. The closer we got to wrapping up this case, the less time I had left with Seb.

I retrieved the tray of cookies, and Seb opened a cupboard and handed me a plate. The comfortable, familiar move reminded me again that he'd spent time here with Nana.

"Honestly, even though I'm leaning more toward Helen"—I moved to the couch to enjoy the cookies in front of the tree—"the only one who seems like he has any real motive is the guy whose relative died at the nursing home. Do you know him?"

"I've only seen him a few times while volunteering."

"Well, if you see him at the Christmas Festival tomorrow, maybe you can point him out."

Seb joined me, sitting so close that his knee touched mine. "If we do see him, we should see if he has an alibi for that night."

"Good call." I nibbled at my sugar cookie, enjoying the buttery crispness.

Seb finished his in two bites and looked around the room with a small smile.

"What are you thinking?"

His cheeks turned a faint pink. "That it's nice not to have to spend a night in an empty house."

My heart twinged for him. "I know it isn't the same, since I never lived here with Nana, but this place is bursting with memories of her. It's bittersweet."

He wrapped an arm around me, and though my heart pounded painfully at the contact, I snuggled in closer. Even if Seb was just being nice—because friends gave friends comforting hugs—I could enjoy this moment of sitting with him in front of the sparkling tree lights.

After a few minutes, I shifted, remembering the pile of Christmas Wishes I needed to go through before Christmas Eve in two days. "Want to watch a movie or something? I have some work to do, but I can do it while we watch."

"I can help," he said. "What are you in the mood for? Something Christmassy?" he asked with a teasing grin.

While I was always down for a Christmas Hallmark movie, I was pretty confident Seb was only saying that to be nice. Plus, the more I thought about how close Christmas was, the more it reminded me that my time with Seb was running out. "I'm in the mood for something else. What's your favorite movie?"

He thought for a moment, his thumb rubbing soft circles on the back of my hand in a way I wasn't even sure he was aware of. "How about *The Fellowship of the Ring*?"

I stiffened, remembering Tate's proposal and our many marathons together.

"Or not." He gave me a quizzical look.

I sucked in a breath. Watching the movie with Seb would be the perfect way to overwrite my memories of Tate, so he would no longer be ruining one of my favorite trilogies. It would be like reclaiming another piece of me from his influence. "Actually, that sounds perfect."

"If you're sure ..."

"I am." I stood and gathered the Christmas Wishes, then got the movie going and we settled in at the couch again. True to his word, Seb helped me check the addresses and the presents.

"How did you get the information for the presents and addresses and everything?" Seb asked as we worked.

"People filled it out with the Christmas Wishes. One star is left to hang on the tree for someone to take and buy the presents, and I keep track of the rest of the information."

"You're amazing, Harp." In the dark, Seb's words were almost like a caress.

At least he couldn't see my blush. "It was María's idea, but I went along with it because I wanted to give back to the community after receiving so much support before."

"We're lucky you came to Whisper Hollow."

I bit my lip and fell silent. When we were alone, it was easy to forget that we were pretending.

Before I knew it, the movie was over, and we'd finished organizing the wishes.

Seb yawned and stretched. "Maybe we shouldn't have started the extended edition so late, but—"

"But if you're going to watch it, you *have* to do the extended edition.'

"Exactly." He flashed a grin at me and stood, then offered me a hand up.

Even now, the simple gesture sent butterflies through my stomach.

"I'm going to do a last sweep of the house, then I'll meet you upstairs."

"Okay." The way he said it made it sound like we were sleeping together, even though he was in a different room. As I made my way up the stairs, I couldn't resist one more glance over my shoulder at Seb as he double-checked to make sure the windows and the front door were locked.

I went to the bathroom and left the door open for Seb, who came in a few minutes later as I was brushing my teeth.

"All clear." He smiled and started to brush his teeth next to me. The feeling was so intimate, so cozy; a part of Seb I never thought I'd get to see, and yet it felt right.

"Thanks again for staying here," I said after rinsing my mouth.

"It's selfish of me," he said. "I never would've been able to sleep if I was worrying about you all night."

And *I* wouldn't be able to sleep with the thought of Seb down the hall. "Well, goodnight."

"Goodnight," he called after me as I fled the bathroom. "Oh, Harp?" He poked his head out of the bathroom door.

"Yeah?"

"I'll leave my door open in case you need anything, or you hear anything."

"Thanks." I closed the door to my room, then leaned against it, trying not to think about how his smile made my heart melt like butter on warm toast.

Yeah. I definitely wouldn't be sleeping tonight.

Chapter 9

Tying the Knot

Despite my restless night, I woke early the next morning to go for a run and work off some of my nervous energy. When I got home, Seb had made cocoa and eggs while I was out.

"I checked around the house, but everything seems normal," he said as we ate.

"Thanks for doing that," I said. "And for breakfast."

"My pleasure."

I had to resist the urge to touch his cheeks, which looked smooth and freshly shaven. "We should probably head into town." I glanced at him. "Do you want to drive together?"

"Sure."

The drive passed quickly—time seemed to do that when I was with Seb—and soon I was back at the shop.

Between thinking about my evening with Seb and our plans to get more info about the murder at the festival, the time for the Christmas Festival snuck up on me.

"You ready to go?" I called to María as I closed the door behind the final customer of the day.

"Just about," she said from somewhere in the back.

While I waited, I gathered the extra Christmas Wishes we'd prepared to take to tonight's party. Since tomorrow was Christmas Eve, we were running out of time to collect presents.

María appeared from the office holding a large package wrapped in shiny wrapping paper and topped with an enormous blue bow. "Here you go."

"What's this?" I felt the inside, which was bulky but light and soft.

"Open it and you'll see."

"We said no presents," I protested even as I unwrapped the package. "You shouldn't have."

Her eyes twinkled, which was never a good sign when it came to María's surprises. "I couldn't resist."

I finished unwrapping it to reveal a pair of matching Christmas sweaters. "Really, you shouldn't have."

She laughed and pulled one sweater from the package and held it up to me. "Well, since you and Sebastian are dating now, I thought you deserved a little something to celebrate."

"These are for Seb and me?" My eyes widened. "I thought they were for us."

"Obviously not." She held up one that was way too large to fit either of us.

"You're having entirely too much fun with this." I looked down at the bright red sweater, which featured two marshmallows on a swing with the words "Kiss me S'more" written underneath them in curling gold script.

"Or you're not having enough fun." She pulled the other sweater from the package and held it in front of herself, her grin widening. Seb's matched mine, but his was green. "Oh, these are even better than I imagined. I was worried yours would look a bit like the Weasely sweaters from Harry Potter, but these colors are much more vibrant."

"I can*not* ask Seb to wear this." Even though it would be a tiny bit cute.

"Why not?"

"It'd be like announcing to the entire town, 'Hey, look at us. We're dating now.'"

María put the sweater back in the bag. "First of all, didn't you already do that when you shared the news with Nancy? And second of all, isn't that sort of the point? The more people who believe you, the better off you are with Tate."

"I'll wear mine, but I won't ask Seb. It's too embarrassing." I walked behind a bookshelf and swapped sweaters.

"That's okay. You don't have to," María said as the front door opened and Seb walked in. "I already did."

He looked between us, his gaze lingering on the sweater in María's hands and the one I wore.

"What do you think?" María asked.

"They're, um, very colorful."

I tugged on the edge of my sweater and walked closer to María. "You don't have to do this. María was joking."

"No, I was—"

I elbowed her in the side to cut off the rest of her sentence.

"That's okay." Seb walked over and took the sweater from her. "I don't mind wearing it."

He raised his arms to pull the sweater over his long-sleeved T-shirt, giving me a glimpse of his chiseled stomach. Who knew carpentry could be so helpful?

"It looks perfect," María said as Seb pulled on his sweater.

"Yeah, perfect," I mumbled around the twinge of disappointment as my view of his stomach disappeared.

María elbowed me, and I tore my gaze away from Seb.

"And you haven't even seen the best part," María said. "Hold hands and I'll show you."

I gave her a look, but before I could say anything, Seb reached over and took my hand, sending a flutter through me.

María reached over and fiddled with the end of our sleeves, then pulled out a red and green string and tied them together so our sleeves joined into a weird sort of sweater-glove thing. "If you tie the knot here, it holds the sleeves together so your hands won't get cold even when you're outside."

"Don't people normally wear gloves for that?" I said as I untied it. We'd look ridiculous walking around tied together.

"Gloves are for people who have no one to hold their hands."

Seb grinned. "You're full of wisdom, aren't you?"

María returned it. "Spend more time over here and you'll learn all sorts of things."

"Are you both ready to go?" I collected the box of Christmas books we'd donated as prizes for tonight's games, trying not to smile at their easy camaraderie. It was nice to see my boyfriend—fake boyfriend—getting along with my friends. Tate wasn't good at that.

"Yeah." María collected the Christmas Wishes and the pens.

Seb walked over and took the box from me. "I'll get those."

"Oh, thanks." My cheeks warmed with a blush, and I wasn't sure if it was from Seb's kindness, these sweaters, or the smirks María kept giving me. I followed them out the door before locking up.

María chatted with Seb the whole walk to Serenity Park while I tried not to focus on the looks we got from people. Was it okay to spread the news like this? Sure, I wanted to convince Tate, but if all of Whisper Hollow thought we were dating, what would that mean once Tate left, the killer was caught, and it was time to break up? No matter how you looked at it, our relationship had a deadline. And if I didn't want to get hurt, I needed to remember that and treat this like the fake relationship it was.

Once we made it to Serenity Park, the crisp air held the scent of pine as well as the tantalizing aroma of roasted chestnuts and cinnamon. Christmas carols filled the air along with the chatter of voices as everyone worked on the finishing touches. Someone had wrapped Christmas lights between the vines and ivy intertwined around the park's wrought-iron gate. And though the oak and maple trees had shed their leaves, bright red bows now decorated their trunks to make up for the lost color. The pine trees held an array of ornaments and shimmered with tinsel and colorful lights.

Booths adorned with festive decorations had been set up throughout the park, creating an aisle in the center lined on either side by giant candy canes. We meandered through the crowds on our walk to the center of the park, where María and I had agreed to set up the Christmas Wishes. Seb's hand brushed mine, and I tried not to react even though electricity jolted through me.

It seemed like most of the town was here; the spaces were packed tightly, with bodies huddled together for warmth as they moved from booth to booth.

"Wow, look at that." María pointed to a life-sized nutcracker standing guard by a booth decorated with a collection of glittering handmade ornaments. The group of older women who'd visited the bookstore earlier that week were looking at ornaments. The one with the white hair and bright cherry lipstick who'd bought the *Ho, Ho, Hoe* book looked to be haggling with the stall owner over the price.

"That nutcracker is nothing compared to that reindeer." I pointed to a huge sculpture of a reindeer grazing on a patch of snow-covered grass next to a booth with handmade scarves, gloves, and hats. I waved at Walter, who stood near the booth, studying a pair of gray-knit gloves. He smiled and waved back, then returned his attention to the gloves as if his life depended on his next purchase.

"I'm not sure why you're focusing on statues when there's all this food around." Seb looked at the food, which ranged from spiced cider to roasted chestnuts, hot chocolate, and gingerbread. His attention lingered on Nancy's stand, which was decorated as adorably as her bakery. She'd even brought her Santa countdown to remind everyone we only had two days until Christmas—as if anyone in this town was capable of forgetting—but neither of those could hold our attention when a towering Christmas tree made of cupcakes with green frosting and edible silver bells stood proudly on display on her central table.

I laughed. "Let's get something to eat once we're done."

We followed the small gravel path, which was already dusted with snow, and moved past the playground, where the happy shouts of children filled the air.

Jessie sat at a bench next to the sheriff, while the kids she babysat played with the sheriff's children on the playground.

"Hey, Jessie." I waved at her as we walked over. "I feel like I haven't seen you in forever."

"It's been a crazy month." Jessie tucked a strand of her honey-colored hair behind one ear, and the bracelets on her wrist jangled. "You know how the holidays are."

"I get it. Things have been wild."

One of the kids screamed, and Jessie sighed. "Speaking of wild, I better check on that."

"Let's plan a girl's night soon," María called after her before turning and interrupting Seb's stare-down with Sheriff Warner by asking, "Any updates about what happened?"

"We're working on some leads."

Of course he kept it vague.

"I heard you found a lighter at the scene of the crime," María said in a conspiratorial whisper.

Seb and I exchanged tense looks.

Sheriff Warner sighed. "How do you know about that?"

María's smile widened. "I have my sources."

"Why do I even bother trying to keep secrets around here?" the sheriff muttered to himself with a shake of his head.

"I guess we should go," María said after a few moments of Sheriff Warner's silence. "We still need to set up the Christmas Wishes."

A large bonfire near the gazebo crackled in the distance, its glow inviting us forward. It was near the main Christmas tree, where we were putting tonight's Christmas Wishes.

"A lighter, huh?" Seb muttered to me. "Seems like something someone who smokes might drop."

I shot him a look. "Yes, it does." Maybe Helen smoked. I hadn't ever smelled it on her, but she could just be one of those people who only did it outside. Didn't most people vape now anyway?

A raised platform had been set up nearby, and someone was performing live Christmas carols, adding to the merry atmosphere.

"Don't you love ice skating, Harp?" María pointed in the distance where figures skated across the pond's frozen surface.

I flushed and looked at Seb, then focused on her. "Yeah, but that's not what we came here for."

"Actually, I can take care of this." María pulled the box from Seb's hands and winked at me. "It'll just take me a few minutes to give the mayor the box for the prizes and put the Christmas Wishes on the main tree. Why don't you two go have fun?"

"We can help," Seb said.

"I insist." María bumped me with her hip and said, "I've got this," before walking off.

We watched her scuttle away, then Seb turned to me. "She seems to want us to go ice skating."

"Yeah, but shouldn't we work on the case?" As more and more clues fell into place, I couldn't help but want to wrap this up quickly. "We should find Helen and Tate."

"I looked for them as we came in. I'm not sure if they're here yet." He looked around, his tall figure easily standing above the crowd to scan for them.

"Should we grab some food, then?" I asked, remembering Seb's longing looks at the food stalls.

"That can wait." He took my hand and pulled me toward the miniature ice rink. "Let's hit the rink."

My cheeks heated, but I couldn't help but smile. We passed the bonfire, where a group of people who were nothing more than fluffy hats and puffy coats roasted marshmallows and sipped cocoa.

"I haven't been ice skating in forever," Seb admitted as we laced up our skates. "Not since I was a boy, and I broke my wrist in a skating accident."

"Ouch." I wrinkled my nose. "Are you sure you still want to?"

He gave me a soft smile. "Yeah, I think it's time to put myself out there again."

I bit my lip and looked down. Seb was a little *too* good at this whole fake dating thing. He made it seem so easy, and like he cared for me as more than just a friend.

We did a slow circle around the rink. While Seb focused on regaining his ice-legs, I admired the twinkling fairy lights and snow-capped trees around us. The cold air nipped at my nose. It was probably as red as Rudolph's, but everything else was perfect.

"Okay, I think I'm good," Seb said after a few minutes.

"If you're sure." I let go of his hand reluctantly.

But he was right. He seemed totally fine again.

He turned and grinned at me. "Like riding a bike, right?"

"Look out!" a boy called as he clipped Seb on the side while skating by way too fast. Seb's arms spun in the air as he fought for balance.

I snagged his hand, but his momentum was too strong, and he pulled me down. We fell in a tangle of limbs, and my breath whooshed out in a pained exhale.

"I guess I shouldn't have let go of your hand." Seb's deep voice rumbled beneath me.

"I guess not," I said with a laugh. Then I turned my head and froze, realizing how close our faces were. His breath mixed with mine in little white puffs, and we stared at each other for a long moment. All I needed to do was lower my head an inch and we'd be kissing.

His warmth seeped into me everywhere we touched, from his broad chest to our legs tangled together. I resisted the urge to lower my head and inhale his musky aftershave.

"Are you okay?" the kid asked from above us.

I blinked and looked around, remembering that we were very much not alone. Flushing, I disentangled myself and stood. "Yes, we are. Are you?"

"I'm fine." The kid shrugged and skated off.

Seb climbed back to his feet. "Sorry about pulling you down. Are you really okay?"

"I think you took the brunt of the fall." I gave him a small smile. "But maybe it's safer if we just keep holding hands."

"Safer for whom?" I thought I heard him murmur as a gaggle of kids skated by, shouting at each other.

We continued for a few minutes in silence. "Harp, there's something I've been meaning to tell you."

"What is it?" My heart pounded at the way he looked at me. I swerved to the side and pulled him with me to avoid that same group of kids from earlier.

A shiver ran down my spine at the strange, sudden sensation of being watched.

I stiffened and looked around, but nothing seemed out of the ordinary. On the other side of the pond, a familiar face caught my eye. Loren was here, and he was staring at me. I gave him a small wave, trying to play it cool. He'd never come back to the bookshop, even though he'd seemed like he wanted to.

Loren waved back, then looked away.

Seb looked around, then straightened. "Do you know that guy?"

"Yeah, why"

"Because that's the man I told you about—the one from the nursing home who got involved in that case with the patient with Tom."

My eyes widened, and I swiveled to face Seb. "That was *Loren*?"

"Yeah. I had no idea you knew him."

"And I had no idea it was Loren you were talking about. We should talk to him." I turned back around, but Loren was gone. I scanned the crowd, searching for his bright red hair and his black coat.

Instead, my gaze landed on Tate, who was walking by the pond. And for some reason, he was with Helen.

Chapter 10

Mistletoe and Murderers

"Tate's here," I said to Seb. It was impossible to mistake him when he wore the beanie I'd given him. "And he's with Helen." What possible reason could they have for being together? And why did Tate look so tense? What could the two of them possibly have to talk about?

"What?" Seb looked around again, then his eyes narrowed.

"That's weird, right?" I asked. "It's not just me."

He shook his head, his jaw tense. "It's not just you."

"Wait, didn't you want to say something?"

"I'll tell you later. This is our chance to get some answers."

We moved to the edge of the pond and quickly exchanged our skates for shoes. Seb took my hand, and we fought our way around the lake's circumference in the direction of the bonfire.

"Want some hot cocoa?" a woman at a small stand asked us as we neared the bonfire and the stage.

"Oh, uh sure." I handed the first cup to Seb before accepting another. "Thank you." The hot cup warmed my chilled fingers. I took a sip of the bitter dark chocolate, then scanned the area for a flash of Helen's dark green coat. With the pond at our back, the stage was now directly in front of us and the bonfire off to the right a bit. "Do you see them?"

"Yeah, they're over there."

Seb tilted his head to where Tate and Helen talked by the bonfire, their beanie-d heads huddled together. The flickering firelight danced off their serious expressions. What were the odds that our two main suspects would be together like this when they had no reason to know each other aside from that brief meeting the night at the bakery?

They said something else, then glanced around covertly and moved so they were standing near the edge of the line of stalls that led almost all the way to the stage.

Seb tugged on my hand in their direction. We made our way toward them, trying to blend in with the crowd as we casually sipped our cocoa. If Tate saw us here, whatever conversation he and Helen were having would be over.

I tried to sift through the chatter of voices around me until I could hear Tate's familiar tenor, but with the happy screams of children, the shouts of the vendors selling their wares, and the band playing "Rockin' Around the Christmas Tree" on the stage, it was almost impossible to eavesdrop.

"We'll have to get closer," I told Seb under my breath.

He tightened his grip on my hand, and we tossed our empty cups into a nearby trash before delving into the crowd.

"There's a spot over there," he muttered to me. "It might work."

We moved into the small stand under a little archway decorated with red bows, which was conveniently just a few feet away from Tate and Helen. They were huddled together again, clearly trying not to be overheard. As long as they didn't turn around, they wouldn't see us. Thankfully, they seemed intent on their conversation and little else.

"Did anyone see?" Helen's question drifted to us through the crowd.

"No, I don't think—"

A roar of approval drowned out the rest of Tate's reply as a new group took the stage and started to play "Jingle Bell Rock." Once the music started up, most of the other conversations died down, but Helen and Tate just put their heads together and kept talking.

"What are they talking about?" Seb whispered to me.

I jumped as his warm breath tickled my ear. I hadn't even noticed him get that close. "I don't know."

Seb gave me a curious look, then focused on their conversation again.

He was too close. Acting too casual. Too handsome. It was all too much. Between what happened on the ice rink and now, I wasn't sure if I was cut out for this fake girlfriend stuff. I wasn't good at keeping my feelings separate from reality.

"It isn't real," I reminded myself under my breath. And I didn't want it to be real. Being in a real relationship was a sure way of getting hurt again. If I let myself, I could fall for Seb all too easily, which was stupid when he'd already told me about his past and how he wasn't ready for a relationship. I was asking for heartbreak.

"Did you say something?" Seb glanced at me.

I shook my head and focused on the other couple.

"Are you sure this is a good idea?" Tate said in a low voice. "If anyone found out ..."

"We won't let them find out. It's too late for regret."

Tate clenched his hands at his sides. "They'd better not. I'm running out of chances."

I chewed on my lip, wondering what they were talking about. It sure sounded like they had something to hide, but we'd need to wait and see if they said anything else.

The song ended, and as the crowd's applause started up, Tate stiffened and looked around.

Seb swore and turned away, putting his back to Tate and his face to me. He towered over me, one hand leaning against the wall behind me, effectively hiding both of our faces from Tate.

"Nice thinking," I said even as my heart took off again and I stared at his lips. My stupid heart. Didn't it know there was no time for romance when we were investigating a murder?

After a few moments, I glanced under Seb's arm. Helen and Tate had moved a little ways away, farther from the crowd and closer to the line of cloth stalls. Considering neither of them were looking this way, they probably hadn't spotted us just now. "Looks like we're safe for now."

"Well, well, well," someone said from behind us. "Look at you two."

We both spun around to find Nancy watching us with a smile almost as big as the cinnamon rolls she served every morning in December.

Under her knowing gaze, I instinctively took a step away from Seb.

"Oh please, don't let me interfere." Nancy's grin widened, reminding me too much of María.

"Interfere with what?" I asked with a smile. Had she realized we were eavesdropping? If it was that obvious, we were in trouble.

"Don't play coy now. I know exactly where you're standing and what's going on with this little clandestine meeting of yours."

"What are you talking about?" I looked around, but the crowd surrounded our tiny little gazebo on either side and the temporary stage was in front of us with the bonfire to our right. There wasn't anything particular that would explain why she watched us with such satisfaction.

Nancy pointed over our heads. "You can pretend all you want, but we all know it's no coincidence that you're standing directly under the mistletoe."

"What?" I glanced up, and nerves exploded in my stomach. Sure enough, there was a sprig of vibrant green leaves with red berries hanging over us and tied with a red ribbon.

Seb glanced at me as if gauging my reaction.

"I already saw you earlier." Nancy winked at me with a wide smile. "You were all over each other a moment ago when you thought no one was looking, so what's the point in acting shy now?"

My face was probably about as red as the berries over my head, but it was hard to know what was worse: Nancy's scolding or Seb's hesitation. He didn't want to kiss me. Of course, Nancy had seen the moment Seb got close to hide us from Tate. She had the most incredibly unfortunate timing.

I looked away, just then noticing that a few people were watching the exchange. *Tate* was watching, but he wasn't standing with Helen anymore. We'd missed our chance to hear the rest of their conversation.

I tugged on Seb's sleeve and glanced his way briefly, hoping he'd get the message.

He slowly angled his head to face me, and my heart pounded in my chest as his eyes met mine. The soft glow of the lights from the stage made his eyes somehow seem brighter and darker, and my cheeks flushed at the look he was giving me.

Seb cupped my face in both of his large hands, his tender touch sending a shiver down my spine. The sound of my pounding heart grew deafening as the air grew charged with anticipation.

Slowly, as if giving me plenty of time to move away, he leaned down. But as his lips drew nearer to mine, I couldn't move, or even breathe. All I could do was stand there and try not to have a heart attack.

Seb pressed his lips against mine in a kiss as gentle and mesmerizing as the flutter of snowflakes.

My eyes slipped shut, and everything else fell away. There was no Nancy, no Tate, no staring crowd, and no Christmas festival. Just me and Seb and the way he softly pulled me closer and deepened the kiss.

Our mouths seemed to fit together as if they were two halves of a poem, nice on their own but perfect together. Seb's hand found its way to the small of my back, and I wrapped a hand around his neck and knotted my fingers in his hair.

His kiss was a perfect blend of innocence and desire, passion and sweetness, caution and dominance. Our breaths mingled, warm and sweet, as the kiss lingered.

Seb pulled back and rested his forehead against mine. His gaze locked on mine searchingly, and I couldn't look away. Being in Seb's arms was like nothing I'd ever experienced before. It was like curling up by the fire and reading a book with Nana. Or watching terrible reality TV shows with Grace while we gorged ourselves on Gushers and Sour Patch Kids. Or spending an evening with my parents.

Seb felt like home.

"Sorry," he mouthed to me before pulling back.

At that, the daydream shattered and fell to pieces around my feet. How could I have forgotten? His apology made it abundantly clear that he'd kissed me to keep up the ruse, not because he'd wanted to. None of this was real—especially that kiss, no matter how much it had felt like it.

"You two are so cute I can hardly stand it." Nancy sighed.

"Oh, we aren't—" I caught myself before saying anything revealing. What would I say anyway? No, I'm not attracted to Seb? That was even more of a lie than our relationship. How could I not be when he stood there, so tall and proud and not the least bit aware of how adorable he looked in his Christmas sweater? With his dark hair curling out from under the beanie he'd put on and covering the tips of his ears and his dark stubble covering his cheeks, it was impossible to tell if he was as flustered as me.

But even more embarrassing than him kissing me in front of everyone was the fact that all it had taken was one kiss for me to forget it was fake. The only reason he was doing this in the first place was to help me with Tate.

Wait a minute. Tate!

I scanned the crowd and found him standing a few feet away with his jaw clenched and his hands curled into fists at his sides. Clearly, he'd seen the kiss too.

"Well, I'd better get back to work." Nancy gave us one more satisfied smile. "Have fun the rest of the night, you two."

"Thanks," I mumbled.

As soon as she walked off, Tate stomped forward.

"What's the meaning of this, Harp?"

Seb stiffened and I put a hand on his arm and said, "Why are you acting so surprised? You know I'm with Seb now." My voice was pleasantly steady, proving I was more over Tate than I'd thought.

"I thought you were going to give me a chance." His gaze darted between our matching Christmas sweaters, and a muscle jumped in his jaw.

"No, that's just something you decided on your own. I told you I'm not interested."

His gaze flicked between us, and his body radiated tension. Way more tension than watching a simple kiss deserved.

Not that anything about that kiss had been simple.

I cocked my head to the side and studied Tate. He was jumpy and anxious, more like he'd been in the early days of our relationship before he'd quit smoking. While he still didn't smell like smoke, maybe Seb was right. "Tate, are you smoking again?"

"What? No."

While I wanted to believe him, his word didn't mean as much as it used to.

"I saw you earlier."

"Why didn't you say anything?"

"You were with someone—a woman." I tried to pretend like I didn't know Helen to gauge his reaction. What was going on with him to make him so tense?

Tate's eyes widened slightly, but then he smoothed his expression. "If you're so *un*interested, why are you asking about who I was with?"

My flush deepened, but I couldn't tell him the real reason I'd been watching him.

A pause fell between us as we studied each other, and Seb's pressure on my hand made it impossible to forget his reassuring presence beside me.

"So why were you talking to that woman?" Seb's voice was hard, and Tate flinched.

"I accidentally ran into her, and we realized we'd seen each other outside the bakery the other night so we talked for a minute, but then she left." Tate returned his attention to me. "Believe me, Harp, it was nothing."

How could I believe him when he'd already lied to me again? Nothing about him had changed. Instead of the familiar pain, the thought just brought a wave of sadness.

"I really need to talk to you, Harp." Tate fidgeted with the sleeve of his coat.

"Whatever you need to say to her, you can say to both of us," Seb said.

Tate clenched his teeth. "Fine, I'll catch you later." He stormed off before I could say anything else.

"What are you doing? This could be our chance to find out what's going on," I hissed to Seb, whose entire body was one ball of tension next to me.

"You think I'm going to let you talk to him alone?" he ground out.

Was Seb jealous?

"He could be a murderer, Harp."

Ah, so it was just his protective instincts kicking in.

I squeezed his hand softly. "He's not going to open up in front of you."

"Then we'll figure out a way for you to talk to him and make sure that you're safe," Seb said.

I nodded, then turned and caught one last glimpse of Tate's back before he disappeared into the crowd.

He and Helen were hiding something, and we needed to find out what.

Chapter 11

Claus on Pause

The next morning, I got up early to make breakfast as a thank-you. I fed Jiji, then took my time getting ready, keeping an ear out for noises upstairs to warn me of Seb waking up, before heading to the kitchen.

A creaking upstairs warned me I needed to hurry, so I whisked the eggs in the frying pan more, as if that would help them cook faster. The smell of cinnamon rolls filled the air, and my stomach grumbled, but I couldn't help but smile as I imagined Seb's surprised reaction.

The front door jiggled.

I froze, spatula in hand.

Someone was trying to get in. Just like Seb thought, someone was outside. Instead of alerting the intruder that I knew they were there, I whispered up the stairs, "Seb?"

No answer.

The doorknob moved again.

"Seb!" I held the spatula in front of me with a shaking hand.

The door swung open before I made it out of the kitchen, and I screamed.

"Whoa! You okay?" Seb rushed inside and took the spatula from me before pulling me into a hug.

The tension dropped from me like snow falling off a tree branch. I leaned against him and inhaled shaky breaths.

"I thought you were asleep and someone was breaking in."

"I'm sorry. I didn't mean to scare you."

"What were you doing outside?" My voice came out muffled against his chest, and I breathed deeply, soaking in his musky scent.

"I wanted to scrape our windshields. You got up too early yesterday, and I missed my chance." He sniffed the air. "Are you cooking something?"

I pulled away and rushed to the stove. "The eggs!"

"They look great," he said as he joined me, even though it was a lie. They were black on the bottom.

I sighed. "Sorry. I just wanted to say thank you for yesterday."

"This is great." He took off his coat and hung it on the back of his chair, then slipped off his shoes. Snow dusted his hair, making it glisten in the morning light.

I filled our plates with bacon, toast, and burnt eggs and tried not to stare as he poured us both a glass of juice. But Seb in pajamas with bare feet and mussed hair was a sight I could get used to.

We chatted while we ate, then he helped me with the dishes.

"I have a few errands to run today," Seb said as he dried a dish I handed him, "so I thought we could drive separately."

"Okay." I finished the last of the dishes, trying to hide my disappointment.

"Be careful outside," he said. "The roads are slick."

I grinned at his warning, thinking of my parents. How many times had they done the dishes together, Dad worrying about Mom while she was out, or Mom kissing Dad goodbye at the door?

Not that I would be kissing Seb goodbye. Of course, my thoughts darted to yesterday's kiss, and I flushed. "I will." I turned to the door to hide my red cheeks.

He walked me over and watched while I got into my car, then went back inside to get ready. Jiji jumped in and settled on my lap.

Grace called as I pulled onto Main.

"Hey, what's up?" Careful of the ice that came with last night's freeze, I navigated the streets slowly. Jiji's claws flexed on my pants as she stared out the window at the giant blow-up Christmas decorations in the yards we passed.

"I wanted to hear about the Christmas Festival last night," she said. "I thought you'd call."

"Seb was over, remember?"

"Ah, right." Her smirk was evident in her tone. "And how was that?"

"It was... fine." I fought to keep my voice even despite the myriad of emotions coursing through me.

"What's wrong?"

"Why do you think something's wrong?"

Grace made a thoughtful noise. "You have that tone."

"What tone?"

"*That* tone." She sighed. "I don't know how to explain it. It's just your ruffled tone."

"I am ruffled." I stroked Jiji once, then returned my hand to the wheel. "Tate might somehow be involved in Tom's murder, and Seb kissed me in front of half the town last night." And I was worried my feelings for Seb were becoming more real than our relationship, but I couldn't say that to Grace. It would provide a world of "I Told You So's." Plus, it was more than a little embarrassing how she always seemed to know me better than I knew myself.

Grace whistled. "Wow, that's a lot to unpack at once."

"You're telling me." All the details from last night spilled from me in a rush while I gripped the wheel tightly and squinted ahead. The road itself was relatively clear, and the morning sun glinted blindingly off the snow. "And to top it all off, I have no idea what to get Seb for Christmas."

"Good luck with that. Finding presents for men is impossible."

"What are you getting Jeff?"

She sighed. "Socks maybe. Or hunting stuff."

"You are absolutely zero help. I'm not getting Seb socks." I sighed as I pulled into the parking lot behind Whispering Pages. "Anyway, I better go. I just got to—oh, crap."

"What?" Her voice was instantly alert.

"Tate's here again." I banged my forehead lightly against the steering wheel. This was the last thing I needed right now. "Maybe I can sic María on him when she gets here. She can be surprisingly fierce when she wants to."

"Harp?"

"Yeah?"

Grace hesitated. "I know you said you've moved on, but I don't think you've really moved past Tate the Lying Cheater, and I don't want him messing up whatever you might have with Seb."

"There's nothing to mess up with Seb." My finger drifted to my lips as I remembered our kiss.

"But there could be." She sighed. "Look, I'm not saying Tate the Lying Cheater isn't a total idiot, but maybe you need to forgive him."

"Forgive him? After what he did to me? Why would I do that for him?" I clenched the steering wheel and leaned my seat back to hide in case Tate looked my way. Instead, I stared at the mural of Serenity Park painted behind the shop, but it brought too many memories of last night. Seb accidentally pulling me on top of him on the ice. His breath mingling with mine. When he ducked his head to hide us. His devastating kiss.

I looked away.

"First of all, forgiveness isn't the same as condoning what he did," she said. "And secondly, you wouldn't do it *for* him. You should forgive him for yourself."

I pursed my lips. "What does that even mean?"

"Haven't you ever heard that not forgiving someone is like drinking poison and hoping the other person dies from it?"

"No."

"Huh. Well, it's a common-ish saying," Grace said. "The point is that you might need to let it go."

María knocked on my driver's side window and I jumped. She grinned, then rubbed her gloved hands together.

"I better go. María is here, and we have a lot of work to do with the Christmas Wishes."

"Good luck today, Harp. Think about what I said."

"I will. Thanks." I hung up and raised my seat slowly, glancing at the front door. Thankfully, Tate was gone. I opened the door with a relieved sigh, letting the chilly air snake into the car's warm interior and distract me from Grace's advice.

María breathed on her gloved hands. "Ready?"

"Definitely. Let's get going." I let us into the shop's warm glow, Jiji and María on my heels. As we did the opening routine, I glanced at the top of one of the shelves where Tate's ornament should've sat, but it was gone. "Did you move that glass book?" I asked María.

"No, why?"

I looked around the shop but didn't spot it. "Because it's gone." A small shiver ran down my spine. Although I had no idea what that ornament had to do with my stalker, I couldn't help but wonder if it was somehow related. Had they been in the shop? My breathing sped at the thought, but I bit my lip instead of saying anything to María. No need for both of us to be freaked out.

Maybe I was overreacting. It could have been Tate, maybe. But I wasn't sure why he'd want to take it back after making such a big deal out of the fact that I still had it.

María and I grabbed the presents, which were wrapped in a variety of wrapping paper featuring everything from reindeer, to red and green stripes, to giant Santa faces, from under the tree. A minute later, we began mapping out the best route for tonight. The monotonous work helped take the edge off my nerves.

"So how was it?" María said after a minute.

"How was what?" I didn't look up from the address I was checking. "The kiss."

My hand jerked, leaving a streak of ink on the paper. "You and Nancy have entirely too much time to gossip."

"Oh, please," she said. "From what I heard, half the town saw it. Go big or go home, right?"

"It was fine." As if there was an adequate word for a kiss that made my toes curl.

"Not from what I heard." She wiggled her eyebrows at me and ran the edge of a pair of scissors down a ribbon to curl it, then pushed that present aside to grab another. "It also sounds like Tate wasn't too pleased by the kiss."

"That reminds me, I saw him and Helen at the festival together last night."

María gasped. "Are you serious?"

"I don't know what they were doing, but they were talking about something they didn't want overheard." I took a moment to fill her in on Helen and Tate's conversation. "He has the gall to get mad at me for kissing Seb and then say he needs to talk to me."

"About what?"

"I don't know. He seemed a little frantic."

"Do you think they were talking about Tom's murder?" María asked after a moment. "You definitely shouldn't meet with him alone. I don't trust him."

"I can't figure out what else it could be about, since I have no idea how they even know each other, but, to be honest, I don't know that I can picture Tate killing someone." But Jiji had hissed at him when he'd come to the store, and she had an instinct for these types of things.

I stopped and shook my head. What was I thinking? I couldn't base murder accusations on who Jiji did and didn't like. If the verdict was up to my antisocial cat, half the town would be in jail by now.

"What if they staged it to look like an accident, but it was a lover's quarrel and Tom ended up getting killed?"

"I suppose that's possible, but where does Tate come in?"

"Oh, oh." María's eyes lit with excitement—a morbid excitement, but excitement nonetheless. "What if they killed Tom for his life insurance?"

"I think you're getting farther away from the truth. What would either of them benefit from that?"

"Hmm ... maybe Helen wanted to get rid of Tom so she can be with Seb but you're in the way, so she needs Tate to woo you."

"And we're back to not even close," I said. "Besides, I'm not convinced the stalking is related to the murder." Unless Tate had done the stalking, and Helen was the one who killed Tom. Or maybe they killed him together, and we just had to discover their motive. Or maybe it was Loren, after all.

"Speaking of Helen, did you know she came in and dropped off a present for a Christmas Wish yesterday?"

"No." I gaped at her, having a hard time picturing Helen doing something nice, but then again, there was probably a lot about her that I didn't know.

The front door swung open and María and I hid the presents we were working on in case a kid walked in. Except it wasn't a kid; it was Seb, and he didn't look happy.

"What's wrong?" I asked.

He glanced around as if making sure the three of us were alone in the shop. "Remember that paper you found outside your house and in the alley?"

"Yeah."

"Turns out it's part of a cigarette pack—a specific brand." He held up a picture he'd printed out. "I took the wrapper you gave me to the police, and the cops said they found traces of it at the crime scene."

My stomach dropped. "Are you saying ..."

"Yes," Seb said. "There's no doubt about it anymore. Whoever has been following you is connected to Tom's murder."

"That doesn't make any sense." I rested my hands against the counter to stop them from shaking. "I barely even know Tom. Why would the killer be following me around?"

As if sensing my distress, Jiji wove between my ankles and meowed up at me. I bent down to pick her up and cradled her against my chest.

"I don't know." Seb took a step closer. "But I don't like it. Can I install some security cameras outside your place? The police agreed it would be a good idea."

"That would be great. Thanks." Seb was always thinking of ways to help others, like how he still volunteered at the nursing home every week. "So, you told them I was being stalked?"

"Yeah, they said they'd send a squad car around your house every hour or so during the night until this is wrapped up. I told them everything you told me, but they said if you think of anything else, you should talk to Sheriff Warner."

"Okay."

María looked between us with wide eyes. "Maybe we should cancel the Christmas Wishes deliveries."

"No." I straightened and sucked in a deep breath to calm my fluttering heart. "Don't be silly. We'll be fine."

"If you're being stalked by a murderer, I don't think going around town delivering presents is the smartest move," María said.

"Sheriff Warner also promised an officer would be over here soon to follow at a distance while you two did your deliveries."

"That's good, but even if it's true that someone is following me, do you really think they'd try to do anything when I'm with others?" I put Jiji down on the counter and picked up the list of names we'd been going through.

"I don't know," Seb said. "I sure don't want to find out though."

"I'm not going to let this person ruin Christmas Eve for all these kids," I said.

María's phone buzzed on the counter, and she read the message, then frowned. "Uh oh."

"What happened?" I asked.

"Santa just canceled. Looks like he accidentally double-booked himself tonight." She looked Seb up and down. "How do you feel about red?"

"Red?" He tilted his head to the side.

"You want Seb to deliver the presents tonight as Santa?" I stared at her with wide eyes.

She scoffed at my expression. "Out of all the things we've talked about, *this* is what you find the most strange?"

"I'll do it," Seb said quickly.

"You don't have to do that," I said. "I'm sure you have things you'd rather be doing."

"I don't." He looked me in the eye. "Besides, I'll feel better if I tag along."

"You're not the one who's going to be tagging along," María muttered, too softly for him to hear. "We just need to find a Santa suit for you to wear."

"I think Nancy has one we could borrow," I said.

"Then let's make this happen, people." María clapped her hands. "It's Christmas Eve, and we've got a lot of children waiting to be surprised."

The next few hours passed in a blur. María finished wrapping and preparing the last presents as Seb tracked down a suit and went to his shop for a bit. I checked the rest of the information, but I couldn't stop thinking about what we'd learned. The silver lining of the somewhat stressful afternoon was that I found a first edition of *The Chronicles of Narnia,* which Seb had told me was his favorite series as a child. Even now, C. S. Lewis was one of his favorite authors. I wrapped it up and put it in my car until I could find a time to give it to him.

Was the killer after me? And if so, why? This wasn't the same as what had happened in October. Even though I'd found Mr. James's body in my shop, I'd never felt as though I were in danger, even while trying to track down the killer. Someone had been trying to frame me, but that was completely different from thinking someone might be trying to kill me.

I shivered and rubbed my hands up and down my arms. Tonight would be fine. We'd be fine. María, Seb, and I would stick together, and Seb was staying the night again. Nothing would happen.

"You ladies ready?" Seb asked as he stepped back into the store a little before closing time with a bundle of clothes in his arms.

"Yeah, we just need to load the presents into the car, and we can head out," I said.

"Let me change and I'll help with that. Oh, and Nancy also had this to go with the outfit." Seb handed me a red bag, then hurried into the bathroom and shut the door.

María walked by humming "I Saw Mommy Kissing Santa Claus" as she flipped the sign on the door to closed and locked up.

"Oh, shut up." I gathered the first batch of presents and shoved them into the red bag Seb had given me, trying to put them in based on the houses we'd be going to first.

A minute later, Seb came out of the shop, dressed in a traditional red velvet Santa coat, which emphasized his broad shoulders. The white faux fur trim around the hem contrasted deliciously with his dark hair, and even the fluffy fake beard he wore couldn't hide his chiseled jaw.

He cinched a black leather belt around his waist, drawing attention to his muscular build, then stepped into the shop.

"This will never work." María studied him.

"What's wrong?" Seb looked down somewhat self-consciously at the black boots covering his feet. The shop's light reflected off their shiny surface.

"Santa is supposed to be fat and jolly, not sexy and smoldering." María walked to a nearby armchair and grabbed a pillow. "Stuff this down your shirt."

Seb pulled up his top enough to stuff the pillow underneath, and I tried not to stare at his flat stomach.

"How's this?" he asked.

I looked up and met his gaze. Based on the mischievous smile playing around his lips, I hadn't done a very good job. "Looks great. Let's go." I didn't glance at him again as we gathered the rest of the presents, which María and I had stuffed into trash bags, and loaded them into the car. María's phone rang, so she walked inside to answer while Seb and I finished with the presents.

A minute later, she hurried over to me.

"Is everything okay?" I asked.

"I just got a call from my mom. She says Abuela has fallen and needs me to take her to the hospital."

"Is she all right?" Seb asked.

"She will be," María said. "But I should go."

I frowned. "Should we go with you?"

"No, that's okay." Her tone was a little too casual. "I just need to swing by urgent care with her. I'm sure it's nothing serious. Sorry to bail."

I took her hand. "It's okay. Leave this to us."

"Have fun." She winked at me when Seb wasn't looking.

Wait a minute. Was she lying about her grandmother to give Seb and me time alone? It was hard to ignore the rather suspicious timing of her excuse.

"I'd better go." María rushed out the door before I could call her out on anything, leaving me alone with Seb and the lyrics for "I Saw Mommy Kissing Santa Claus" still playing in my head.

Chapter 12

All I Want for Christmas is a Not-Fake Boyfriend

A few minutes later, Seb and I made it to the first house. I parked on the street not too far from a single-story brick house. It was probably better for Santa not to show up in a Prius. "Looks like this is for a single mom and her son, Parker." I pointed to the correct present in the pile, one wrapped in shiny blue paper with a silver bow, then double-checked the list. "It's that one. And it looks like Parker asked for some Pokémon toys."

"Leave it to me."

Seb and I climbed out of the car, and he hoisted the bag onto his back, making him really look like Santa. I hung back while Seb walked to the front door and knocked loudly three times.

A few moments later, a small boy who appeared to be around six or seven opened the door.

"Ho, ho, ho. Merry Christmas," Seb said in a deeper voice than usual. "Are you Parker?"

The boy's eyes widened as he took in Seb, and he nodded once.

"It sounds like you've been a good boy this year."

Parker nodded so hard he looked like a little bobblehead figure. "I have been." He flashed a smile at Seb, revealing a missing front tooth. A woman who must've been his mother appeared behind him, and her eyes widened as well. She must not have known that someone had put Parker's Christmas Wish on the tree.

"Good, because I can only give this"—Seb pulled the bag from his back and put it on the floor so he could dig out the blue present and hand it to Parker—"to good little children."

I couldn't help but smile as Parker's face lit up, and when I looked at the mom, there were tears in her eyes.

"Merry Christmas." Seb patted his head and stepped back.

"Thanks, Santa! I'm so glad you got my letter."

"I hope you'll be a good boy next year too."

"I will." Parker's head bobbed again, but then he frowned and looked up at Seb.

His mom stepped forward and put a hand on his shoulder. "What's wrong, honey?"

"No one is going to believe you were really here," Parker said to Seb. "Can I take a picture with you?"

Seb glanced at me over his shoulder, and I shrugged.

"Of course," he said in a booming voice before kneeling next to Parker, who ran over and threw his arms around Seb's neck. The mom quickly snapped a photo.

Parker stepped back and studied Seb. "You're not as old as I thought you'd be."

I choked back a laugh.

"The joy of Christmas keeps me young," Seb said after a moment where I assumed he was fighting for control of his smile.

"Huh." Parker looked up at him, then back down at his present.

"I better go. Lots of children to visit tonight."

Parker shut the door without another word, but even with it closed, I could still faintly make out him ask, "Can I open it now?"

I burst out laughing as we walked back to the car. "The joy of Christmas?"

"I was working on the fly," Seb muttered.

"Sure you were," I teased. The streets, adorned with a light dusting of snow, glistened under the streetlights' soft glow. For a moment, it was easy to pretend like nothing was wrong.

"Too bad we don't have any presents for the nursing home," Seb said. "It's just over there."

I nodded, but my thoughts immediately darted to how Tom was killed not too far from the nursing home. The killer had been in this area.

"Thanks for everything," I said softly to Seb. It was thanks to him that I could go out around town at night and not be scared.

"It isn't a big deal." His footsteps crunched on the frozen ground, which looked like a sea of glittering white compared to the sky's velvety blackness. The trees, stripped bare of their leaves, stood tall and skeletal, their branches etched against the glow of the moon.

"But it is, and I don't think you understand it. Not every guy would be willing to do everything you've done, and I just want you to know how grateful I am for it... for you." It was hard not to compare him with Tate, who was definitely not as service-oriented as Seb. "I enjoy spending time with you, and I'm glad to have someone in my life I know will never lie to me."

At my words, his smile fell, and a strange moment of hesitation flickered across his expression.

The sight caused my chest to tighten.

"Sebastian? Is that you?" someone asked from across the street.

We both looked over to find Helen making her way to us.

"I almost didn't recognize you in that suit, but I heard your voice and knew I was right." She flashed him a bright grin.

"What are you doing here?" I asked Helen in a tone that came off a tad too accusatory.

She flipped her scarf over one shoulder and met my gaze. "I live over there." She tilted her head to the other side of the street, where a group of townhouses huddled together against the cold.

"Oh." Ohhh. *This* was the area where Tom was killed, and Helen just happened to live nearby.

"I could ask you the same question." She looked Seb up and down in his Santa suit. "In fact, I could ask a lot of questions."

Seb took my hand. "We're delivering presents for Harp's Christmas Wish program."

"Oh, that's sweet." She didn't look at me. "And will you be doing that all night?"

Her tone was far too inviting considering she knew I was dating Seb. But since she seemed to have had no problem cheating on Tom and not a lot of regret about it after his death, hitting on someone in front of their girlfriend probably didn't bother her at all. I tried to keep my thoughts toward her generous since she'd provided one of these presents, but it was hard with the way she never stopped smiling at Seb.

"I'll be with Harp all night," he said firmly.

Helen narrowed her eyes but quickly cleared her expression and smiled at him. "That's too bad. You'll miss the Christmas Eve fun."

Even though Seb was only staying with me to make sure I was safe and not because we were a real couple, I couldn't help but be glad that he'd be spending the night with me instead of her.

I still hadn't forgotten how she'd tried to pin Tom's murder on Seb nor how she didn't have a good alibi. Just because the police hadn't found enough evidence to charge her didn't make her innocent.

"What about you?" I tried to keep my tone nonchalant. "Any plans to meet someone tonight? Maybe someone from the Christmas Festival."

Her eyes widened briefly. "Actually, I'm going to a party, so I'm sure I'll see quite a few people from the festival." She stepped forward and rested a hand lightly on Seb's forearm. "If you change your mind, the invitation is open."

"Thanks, but I won't." Seb tugged on my hand, dislodging her grip with the movement. "We'd better go. We still have a lot of deliveries to do tonight."

"Bye, Sebastian," Helen called behind us.

"She's obviously still hiding something." I climbed into the car and slammed my door shut.

"We already suspected that." Seb situated the bag in his lap, then plugged the next address into his phone's GPS. "But being jealous isn't enough of a reason to suspect her of murder."

I flushed and glanced at him as I pulled onto the street. "I'm not jealous!"

"Oh, really?" He laughed and held his hand up, revealing fingers that were slightly white. "Then why were you trying to squash my hand a moment ago?"

"Because ... I don't like her."

Seb flashed me a smile as I turned onto another street, then he sobered. "Let's worry about that stuff tomorrow and enjoy tonight together."

My thoughts darted to the moment of hesitation on his face, but I pushed my doubts aside. Seb wouldn't hurt me or lie. I could trust him.

You thought you could trust Tate, my annoying inner voice reminded me.

I shoved the thought away with monumental effort and focused on the next house, which sat back in a quiet subdivision where icicles glinted on the rooftops of the quaint houses lining the street. A Christmas tree lot sat around the corner, and the scent of pine hung heavy in the air.

On the street across from us, a horse-drawn carriage rolled by, its passengers, a man and woman, snuggled under some blankets. The man leaned down and kissed the woman, then the horse drew them out of sight. The clip-clop of its hooves and the couple's joyful laughter faded into the night.

Seb was just as good with the second kid as he was with the first, and as we went from house to house and child to child, I realized he was right. Watching how sweet he was with the kids, remembering how quickly he'd offered to come and help me tonight, and seeing him with Helen was too much. I couldn't deny it when my jealousy had made everything so clear. I was falling for Seb.

"Hey." Seb waved a hand in front of my face as we walked to the next house near the town square. A few carolers stood around a majestic fir tree that dominated the space, its branches laden with ornaments and twinkling lights. "You all right? You've been pretty quiet the last few houses."

I blinked and looked up at him. "Oh, yeah." But the more time I spent with him, the less okay I'd be. I'd need to extricate myself from this situation as soon as possible. Fake dating someone when my feelings weren't fake had proven too dangerous, and I wasn't going to let myself get hurt again. Especially if he was hiding something from me. "I'm fine." At least I would be once we ended this facade.

The familiar tune of "Joy to the World" rose up from the carolers, and a few people in the crowd joined in, their faces red from the cold. Right now, joy was the last thing I was feeling.

"Are you sure?" Seb's piercing blue eyes still somehow managed to look sexy and concerned even with the white beard he wore.

"I'm sure." My breath misted out in front of me in the chilly air as if trying to draw attention to my lie.

We made it to the house in silence, and Seb switched back into boisterous Santa mode as two children sprinted out with a scream to throw their arms around his waist. The scent of apple cider drifted from the open door, and though the daughter only wore one sock and the son's pajama shirt was buttoned up incorrectly as if he'd rushed out here in a hurry, neither of them seemed to notice as they gazed up at Seb in adoration.

I waited a little ways away, pacing on the sidewalk while I tried to figure out what to do.

A gust of wind blew down the street, rustling the bare branches overhead. I shivered as goosebumps rose on my arms and neck. I glanced around, but no one on the street seemed to be paying attention to me as people bustled by on last-minute Christmas Eve errands.

The glow of a cigarette drew my attention to a dark silhouette leaning against the back of a building on the next street. The cigarette looked like an ember in the black night before it went dark again, but it illuminated a pair of hunched shoulders and a face angled toward the ground.

My heart took off.

Lots of people in town smoked, but so did the murderer. If I could just glimpse whoever was in the alley, I could stop worrying.

I glanced at Seb, who was still busy with the kids, then pulled my hood up to cover my face and crossed the street. The cigarette's ember flickered and wisps of smoke curled upward, gray against the black of the sky.

At his next puff of air, the glow lit his face, revealing sharp angles and enigmatic eyes.

Loren.

Chapter 13

Kiss Me S'more

A few hours later, we drove back to the shop. Not wanting to ruin the spirit of Christmas, I kept my concerns about Loren to myself while we finished the rest of the gift-giving.

"I was thinking I could leave my car at the store tonight, and we could drive back together," Seb said as we made it to Whispering Pages, jarring me from my thoughts.

My stomach dipped with nerves, even though a car ride was nothing to be nervous about. "Yeah, sure." Now that I realized how much I wanted to be with Seb, worry had become my constant companion. What if he didn't care for me like I cared for him? Putting my heart in a vulnerable situation again was a no-go, but every moment I spent with Seb made me like him more.

While Seb changed back into his normal clothes inside the shop, I put the rest of the supplies back in my office, including the Santa bag I needed to return to Nancy later. As I stepped out into the cold again, Jiji appeared from the shadows, her eyes shining in the darkness. I didn't know where she went when she wandered around, but she always seemed to know when it was time to go home.

I glimpsed Walter walking down Main Street toward my shop. Thankfully, he wore the gray gloves he'd been eyeing yesterday because it was frigid outside. The poor guy must've been freezing.

Nancy opened her bakery door and waved Walter in. He ducked through the entrance, and she gave me a wink before closing the door again.

I bit back a smile. That sly fox. If Walter wasn't careful, he was going to be more than a visitor here soon. It looked like Nancy had a thing for him.

Seb joined me and opened my car door. "Everything okay?"

"Yeah, thanks." I slid into the car, my cheeks heating. "I saw a customer from the shop, but he's gone now."

Jiji jumped onto my lap, her purring filling the brief silence. After the last two hours of talking with kids, it was nice to have a minute to sit in silence. We drove for a few minutes in silence while "Jingle Bells" played on the radio. On either side of the road, Christmas lights lining the houses lit up the spaces as if guiding us home.

Seb turned on the heater, warming our frozen fingers as we rode home. My headlights illuminated the snowflakes falling from the heavy clouds that hung over us like a dark blanket. Was there more to Loren than we knew? Maybe Seb would think I was overreacting, but I had to tell him.

I opened my mouth, but Seb beat me to it.

"The last two kids reminded me of Coop and me when we were young." He turned down the music to match his quiet voice. "I miss him."

I swallowed my comment and tried to figure out what to say. "I'm sorry. That must have been hard for you, but I think it's normal to miss your little brother."

His eyes flashed in the darkness as we passed another streetlight. "I miss him, but I'm also angry at him."

"I don't blame you."

Seb reached over and took my hand. The gesture was becoming familiar, though it still wreaked havoc on my pulse. "I want to forgive Coop, but I don't know how."

"It takes time, but I'm sure you'll find a way." I squeezed his fingers.

"So, it's just a matter of time?" Seb sighed. "I was hoping for a faster solution."

"I wish I had one for you, but I think it's especially hard to move on when it's someone we loved who hurt us. But the fact that you want to already shows how much you love him."

Seb was silent for a long moment. "Have you forgiven Tate?"

I took a moment to ponder the question. "I was furious and lonely for the first few months, but now I'm okay. I struggled for so long because I didn't want to forgive Tate. But recently I realized it was possible to forgive Tate without condoning what he'd done, and now things don't seem so bad." I was finally letting go of the poison.

Seb's eyes widened. "You aren't angry anymore?"

"I don't think so." I tried to organize my thoughts, which swirled around my head, much like the snow outside the car. "When he first showed up in town, everything felt fresh and painful again, but the more time I've had, the more I realized that my past got me to who I am and where I am now, and Tate is part of that past."

The clouds dumped buckets of snow on the car, and the squeak of the windshield wipers filled the budding silence.

"Are you glad Tate came to town?" Seb asked.

"I ... never thought of it quite like that, but yeah, I might be. A lot of good came from his visit." I didn't look down at our interlocked hands. "If he hadn't come, I might never have confronted my feelings. I had moved on, but I hadn't let go, and I think that would've continued to hurt me even if I didn't realize it." I also would have kept avoiding my feelings for Seb, but no matter how open we were being now, I didn't want to say that.

"I'm glad you aren't hurting anymore." His voice was warm in the darkness.

I shivered. "Me too. And I know you'll get there."

Seb was silent for a moment, then asked, "If you don't mind me asking, how did you two meet?"

"Tate was the TA in a class I took during my undergrad, and once I finished the class, we kept in touch and eventually, he asked me out." I smiled, remembering how excited I'd been back then.

Seb filled the rest of the drive home with questions about Tate. While I'd given him the abbreviated version a while back, I hadn't told him—or anyone else—all the details. But the more I talked, the more it eased the remnants of the wound in my heart.

By the time we got home, the snow covered the world in crisp white, looking like the fresh start I needed. Seb got out of the car, and I hid his present under my coat, then he opened my door and took my hand so we could traverse the few feet to the front door together.

We walked in, then shook the snow off us as we peeled off our coats and gloves. I was careful to keep his present hidden.

A moment of awkward silence fell between us, and I hurried to fill it before I could think too much about his moment of hesitation. "I know it's not that late, but do you want to go to bed?"

"Do you?" His gaze met mine, and suddenly I could imagine the two of us together and what it would be like to wake up next to him looking at me like that every morning.

My cheeks heated as I realized how my question might have come off. "I didn't mean that as an invitation or anything."

Seb's deep laughter filled the room, chasing away the last bit of stiffness between us. "I didn't think it was, but a guy can hope, right?" He winked at me and walked through the hall to do the same sweep of the houses he'd conducted the last two nights. Jiji trailed after him like a small black shadow.

I watched his broad shoulders as he disappeared around the corner into the living room, then exhaled. What was I doing? Now that I was painfully aware of my feelings, I was making a mess of things.

"I'm going to make some cocoa," I said as he climbed the stairs to check the second floor. "Do you want some?"

"Sounds great," he called down to me. His checking the house every night made me feel safe, especially now that we'd discovered the person following me was connected to Tom's murder.

Once he was out of sight, I shoved his present under the tree, then sprinted to the kitchen.

Seb came back down a few minutes later, wearing a pair of gray sweatpants and a white T-shirt that stretched across his impressive chest, and leaned against the counter. The milk was already warming over the gas stove, but I kept myself busy measuring cocoa powder, sugar, cinnamon, and salt to keep from looking at him.

"How would you feel if I lit a fire?"

"That'd be great. Thanks." I focused on mixing the ingredients before pouring in the milk. It was good to have something to keep me busy.

He went into the other room, and the sound of him throwing logs into the fireplace and crinkling paper filled the space between us. About ten minutes later, he came back in.

"Thanks for your help today," I said to keep the silence from dragging too long. The wind howled outside as the storm picked up strength.

Seb stared outside through the kitchen's frost-kissed windows as the world turned white. "I'm glad I could help."

"You've done plenty of that lately." I forced a laugh to keep my tone light. "I'm sure it'll be a relief for you once you're not on duty."

"Don't say that." He spun around, his expression hardening. "Don't make it sound like you're some sort of responsibility."

I shrank under his glare and focused on keeping the cocoa from boiling over. Even still, I couldn't help but watch him from the corner of my eye. "Sorry."

He ran a hand through his hair and looked down. "No, I'm sorry. I'm not mad at you. I just don't want you to believe that I think keeping you safe is a burden."

I swallowed past the dryness in my mouth. "What do you want me to think?"

"I want you to think you're special and any guy would be lucky to have you."

"*Any* guy?" Did that include him?

"Yes." Seb stepped closer.

Had the kitchen always been that small?

Jiji leaped onto the table with a loud meow.

I jumped and flung the spoon I was using to stir into the air, spewing droplets of steaming cocoa on Seb. "Oh my gosh, are you okay?" I moved the cocoa off the burner, grabbed the towel, and dabbed at his arms.

He caught my hand. "Harp."

My pulse took off at his deep tone. "Yeah?"

"Can I kiss you?"

I froze, one hand still on his bicep as I stared into his blue eyes. How had I not noticed how long his lashes were? Or how his eyes had flecks of green? The silence stretched between us like the caramels Nana used to make at Christmas, and I swallowed.

Kissing Seb would be a terrible idea. It would make me care for him more, which was the opposite of what I needed, considering we'd be breaking up soon. He was still planning on breaking up, right? Or did this kiss mean otherwise? But then why had he apologized after the last kiss?

"But"—my voice cracked, so I cleared my throat—"there's no one else around." No Nancy to convince or Tate to drive away. No one but the two of us.

His eyes darkened, and he cradled my cheek with one hand, brushing his thumb across my cheek. "That's kind of the point."

My breath caught at the contact, while my mind raced to catch up. It was a terrible idea, but how many more chances would I have to treasure my time with him like this? If I could have nothing else, I could at least have this moment. "I suppose it wouldn't be a bad idea to practice."

"Trust me, you don't need the practice." His trademark grin made a quick appearance along with the single dimple in his left cheek. "But I'll take what I can get."

Seb's lips brushed against mine. For a moment, I stood frozen, but then a soft sigh escaped me and a shiver chased through me at his touch.

Seb pulled back enough to look down at me, a wordless question in his eyes. The yearning in his gaze mirrored the fire kindled inside me.

The air around us thickened with anticipation, and my heart pounded with excitement and apprehension.

"I think I need more practice," I murmured as I went up onto my tiptoes to kiss him again. I leaned into him, gripping his t-shirt, seeking refuge in his embrace. Seb would protect me from this storm. He'd protect me from whoever was stalking me. And he'd even protect me from the guy who broke my heart.

He smiled against my lips and snaked one arm around me before pulling me close. His fingers traced a path along the curve of my waist, leaving a trail of heat in their wake.

Seb's touch grew bolder as he pulled me impossibly closer, and through his thin T-shirt I could feel his rock-solid chest and the beat of his heart that echoed my own. I wrapped one arm around his neck and buried my other hand into his hair.

Seb was as good a kisser as he was a listener, if that were even possible.

I sank into the moment, losing myself in the intoxicating scent of his skin, a tantalizing blend of musk and peppermint. His kiss was a sweet fusion of desire and tenderness, each movement filled with a passion that left me breathless.

Jiji gave a loud meow of complaint and jumped on my shoulder, her nails digging into the skin as she fought for balance.

"Ouch." I pulled away from Seb and extricated Jiji from my clothes.

"The power's out." Seb glanced around as if as dazed as I felt.

Jiji jumped onto the counter and started licking herself as if nothing had happened.

But something most definitely had happened. Something as wonderful as it was horrifying—something that still had my heart trying to pound its way from my chest and my cheeks burning.

Avoiding looking at Seb, I used the flickering flames from the fire to make my way around the kitchen table to the wall and try the fuse. "Looks like the storm knocked it out."

"That's not good." Seb joined me by the kitchen door.

"At least you've already got the fire going."

"Hey Harp, about what just happened. I shouldn't have—"

My breath stuttered in my chest, and I turned away. He'd done it again. It wasn't the exact same as an apology, but it might as well have been. My hopes that Seb's feelings were becoming as real as my own turned to ash.

"You don't have to say anything. It's okay." I rummaged through a cupboard to cover the tears stinging my eyes. I found a bag of marshmallows. Turning to Seb, I tried to force a smile. "Too bad I don't have any graham crackers and chocolates. Nana would be ashamed."

He hesitated, something unsaid darkening his eyes. "You don't want to talk about what happened?"

Did I want to talk about how Seb said he shouldn't have kissed me when it was the most perfect kiss of my life? No... I really didn't.

I shook my head. My emotions were far too close to the surface.

"Maybe we can later?"

I gave a noncommittal shrug.

He flashed a hesitant smile. "I never say no to marshmallows and cocoa."

We situated ourselves on the floor in front of the crackling fire.

Seb put two marshmallows onto his skewer and raised an eyebrow in challenge. "Ready for the perfect marshmallow?" The dancing flames reflected off his dark eyes.

"That's pretty big talk." I reached for the bag, trying to let go of my awkwardness. What was I doing letting myself get swept up in things? I knew this was fake, and I'd let myself forget. I wouldn't make that mistake again. But for now, I was wasting precious time with Seb.

"Challenge accepted," I said.

"Speaking of challenges"—he pulled something from his sweatpants pocket, then held out a small package wrapped in shiny green paper to me—"this is for you."

I accepted the present and our fingers brushed. How even that could affect me after the kisses we'd shared was beyond me. "Should I be offended *that* was your segue?"

He laughed, his own lips quirking up at the corners. "It was a challenge to figure out what to get you."

I couldn't look away from his mouth. What if I leaned forward and kissed him again? How would he react? He was sitting so close that it would be easy to do. But then I remembered how he'd just apologized, and I leaned back.

"Are you going to open it?"

Seb's question pulled me from my thoughts, and I yanked my attention from his mouth down to the package in my hands. At least the firelight would hide my blushing cheeks.

"If we're doing presents now..." I grabbed his present from where I'd hidden it and handed it to him. "This is for you. You go first."

"If you're sure." He hefted the package as if weighing it, then held it up to the fire as if he could see through it. Finally, he held it to his face and sniffed it.

I laughed. "Just open it, you weirdo."

He pulled out *The Chronicles of Narnia.* "I love this series."

"I know. You told me."

He grinned and nudged me. "Okay, your turn."

I opened the package to reveal a small pepper spray bracelet. With a laugh, I put it on. "Is this you making fun of me for the way we met?"

His smile edged with worry. "After seeing how effective it was on me, I figured you could wear it until the situation with this stalker gets resolved. That way, I won't worry about you so much." He rubbed the back of his neck. "I know it's not very romantic, but—"

"Actually, it's perfect." And it really was. Seb's gift showed he'd been thinking about me just as much as I'd been thinking about him.

I slid the bracelet onto my wrist, and the playful atmosphere shattered as quickly as it had come.

"We still need to figure out what to do about Tate and Helen," he said. "I was thinking I could try to get the truth out of Helen since she's probably less dangerous."

"We don't know that. She could be the one who shot Tom," I said before my logic caught up to my jealousy. "But speaking of the stalker, I should mention I saw Loren smoking outside the motel when we were doing deliveries today."

"Are you questioning his alibi?"

"I don't know."

Seb fell silent and stared into the flames as if the answers were hidden in their dancing sparks. The weight of our situation pressed down on me.

"I think I should talk to Tate first." I tried to keep my voice steady despite the unease sitting on my chest like Jiji loved to do. "He seemed pretty desperate to talk to me alone."

Seb stiffened. "Desperate and alone are two of the last words I'd like to put with you and Tate."

Butterflies fluttered to life again in my stomach at his tone.

"Maybe you could meet at Nancy's. She always stays open until noon on Christmas Day to give families a place for a Christmas breakfast."

"That's nice of her." But it also made me sad. She probably didn't want to be home on her own, and none of her children had come to visit. I pushed that worry away for another time.

I pulled out my phone to text Tate, but Seb rested a hand over mine.

"Is that how you want to spend Christmas?"

After a moment's hesitation, I nodded. "I'd rather get this resolved sooner rather than later." Even if it meant the end of these moments with Seb.

He was quiet for a long moment, and the crackling flames filled the silence for me. "All right. Let's do it."

I shivered and sent off the message.

Almost immediately my phone buzzed a reply.

I'd love to meet you on Christmas! I've been hoping you'd reach out. Just tell me when and where.

I sent a quick response, then put my phone away, not wanting to think about why Tate hadn't even gone home for Christmas. Was he truly that desperate to see me? What did he have to do with the murder?

"With the power off, it'll be way too cold to sleep upstairs tonight." Seb wrapped the blanket from the couch around me, pulling me from my thoughts.

I licked my lips and glanced at the crackling fire. "Should we ... should we sleep in front of the fire?"

He turned to me, but I stared at the dancing flames instead. The silence seemed to last an eternity before he spoke. "That would probably be for the best."

What did his careful tone mean? Did he not want to sleep down here? Maybe I shouldn't have suggested this. It was obvious he regretted that kiss.

Seb stood, back turned. "You can have the couch if you want. I'll get some blankets and pillows."

"You don't have to do that. Nana has some sleeping bags we can use, and I can grab some blankets." At his wide-eyed look, I hurried to add, "It doesn't seem fair to have me on the couch if you're on the floor. Let's both sleep there."

He seemed too surprised to object, so I took the moment to retrieve the sleeping bags. Once I was alone, I let out a breath.

That was close. The moment of insecurity reminded me that while I wanted to treasure my time with Seb, I couldn't allow the lines to blur any more than they already had. Time was running out, whether I was ready or not.

Seb would never break my heart like Tate, and losing him, even in this fake relationship, would hurt much worse. Seb had become my best friend, but with every moment we spent together, I was sure I couldn't go back to being just friends. Even the thought of it hurt. But no matter how much I wished otherwise, our time pretending grew shorter the closer we got to solving this case, and every time he apologized for kissing me just convinced me friendship was what he wanted. He'd let himself get carried away now, but he obviously regretted it.

As much as I trusted Seb to protect me, I couldn't trust him not to hurt me. I'd already given him far too much of my heart for that, and all I could do now was enjoy what time we had left together before it ended.

Chapter 14

This Christmas I'll Give You My Heart

I snuggled into my pillow to block the morning light telling me to get up and go for a run. My bed was too warm and comfortable to get up. Jiji meowed, her soft purr vibrating against my back where she'd settled last night. Without even moving, she seemed to sense the moment I woke up, and she meowed.

I started to stretch, and an arm around my middle flexed and pulled me closer with a groggy murmur.

My eyes flew open, giving me a close-up view of a white T-shirt, the dark stubble on Seb's jaw, and his slightly parted lips before he nuzzled his face into my hair. Heat flooded my cheeks, and I forced my eyes closed again, feigning sleep while I figured out what in all that was Middle Earth was going on right now.

The power had gone out last night, so we'd slept in sleeping bags in front of the fire. That part checked out and made sense.

So how had I ended up with Seb's arms around me, our legs tangled together, and me using his quite muscular chest for a pillow? Our sleeping bags were such a mess that I couldn't even tell whose we were in.

To quell the panic rising in me, I tried to match my breathing to the steady rise and fall of Seb's chest. It seemed like he was still asleep, so maybe I could get out of this situation with him none the wiser.

Even still, my racing heart seemed to announce to the entire room exactly how awake I was—awake and aware of every place Seb and I were touching. One of my hands rested on the soft cotton of his shirt, but it was nothing to how one of his arms curled possessively around me, his heat bleeding through my sleep shirt.

I had to get out of this sleeping bag before I spontaneously combusted. That was a thing, right? With someone like Seb it should be. He needed to come with a warning label: caution. Too sweet and attractive for his own good. Do not let loose near any females ages twenty to forty.

Apparently done being patient, Jiji climbed across my chest and forced herself into a non-existent space between Seb and me.

"Jiji, no!" I whispered, but it was too late.

Seb's eyes popped open as Jiji stepped on him, and his arm tightened around me once more, as if it were instinctual to hold me close, but then his gaze met mine and he released me. "I'm so sorry."

His voice was rough with sleep and somehow unbelievably sexy.

Which was the last thing I should be thinking, considering he'd sort of friend-zoned me.

"That's okay." But even if I had been the one who'd snuggled with him in my sleep, he'd still put his arm around me. Did that mean anything? No, wait. Why would it when he'd just apologized for kissing me last night?

I forced a laugh to try to cover the awkwardness, though it was probably impossible for him *not* to notice how red my cheeks were. "I guess sleeping next to each other on the floor wasn't a good idea."

The only one who seemed oblivious to the strain was Jiji, who curled up in a ball and made a place for herself in the warm nest of blankets we'd abandoned.

"Merry Christmas?" he said it like a question. Not as if he wasn't sure of the date but as if he wasn't sure what to say to me.

Which was the last thing I wanted. I needed to pretend like everything was fine and normal.

"Merry Christmas." I climbed to my feet and started tidying the blankets. Not that it felt like Christmas with us planning to confront my ex, who may or may not have been involved in a murder. Part of me wanted to put off this talk with Tate to prolong my time with Seb, but the rest realized what a terrible idea that would be. I was already in too deep. I needed to get out now before I lost all hope of recovering.

Seb got to work beside me, rolling our traitorous sleeping bags back up.

"Do you still want to do this today?" he asked after a few minutes.

I swallowed back my hesitation and fear. "We need to." I couldn't keep living with this threat hanging over me, and I didn't want Seb to have to keep pretending anymore.

"All right," he said heavily.

We got ready in silence, Seb throwing on a pair of glasses and a beanie in a terrible excuse for a disguise, before heading to Sugarplum Delights.

"Let's go over the plan once more," Seb said as I pulled into a parking spot.

I turned my car off. "I need to tell Tate that I saw him with Helen and find out what they were talking about the night of the Christmas Festival."

"And if you want me to call the police, you—"

"Tap my cell phone, I know." I smiled at him to soften my teasing.

He sighed. "Okay, I'll be close enough to be there if you need something but far enough away that I don't attract Tate's notice."

I tapped the book in his lap, *The Hitchhiker's Guide to the Galaxy*. "I'm sure you'll blend in perfectly."

He gave me a crooked smile, though worry filled his blue eyes. "I'll go in first and claim a table."

"Sounds good. I'll wait until Tate arrives, then I'll follow him in."

For a long moment he looked at me, and in the confined space of the car, my heartbeat sounded extra loud.

"You okay?" I asked after a minute.

Seb leaned across the space between the seats and gave me a soft kiss on the cheek. "Be careful, Harp." And then he was gone. Somehow, that didn't feel like it was what Seb had wanted to say.

I waited a few minutes until Tate walked into the bakery, then I got out of the car and headed to Sugarplum Delights. Before I got inside, someone called my name.

"Harper!"

I turned to find Loren making his way down Main Street toward me.

"Merry Christmas, Loren."

"Merry Christmas." He smiled at me, his nose red from the cold. "I'm glad I caught you today."

"You are?"

"Yeah, I've been hoping to find the right time to ask, but honestly it never feels like the right time, so I'm just going to call this a Christmas miracle and do it." He sucked in a deep breath. "Would you go out with me?"

I blinked at him. "What?"

"I want to take you on a date," he repeated slowly, the tips of his ears turning red to match his nose. "Is that okay?"

"I'm sorry. I'm dating Seb."

He sighed. "I had heard that, but I was hoping it wasn't true." He gave me a rueful smile. "But I figured I'd regret not asking more than I'd regret being turned down."

"I'm flattered, but I can't." Was that why he'd been hanging around?

"Well, it was worth a shot." He gave me another wave and continued down the street, his hands in his pockets.

I did my best to brush off the unexpected encounter and pushed open the door to Sugarplum Delights. Upon entering, I inhaled the warm scent of cinnamon and sugar mingling with the rich aroma of brewing coffee as I scanned the interior.

Nancy waved at me from behind the counter, but she was talking to another customer. A young family sat at one of the window booths. The mom grabbed one of the little boy's hands before he could catch hold of the poinsettia sitting as a centerpiece and said, "Santa is still watching."

I waved at Mr. Humphrey and Lillian, who were enjoying a hearty breakfast of bacon, eggs, and cinnamon rolls. Seb had claimed an empty seat and sat with his head down, his book open in front of him on the table while he sipped from a mug of what was probably peppermint tea. I let my gaze skim over him so as not to draw any attention to his presence and found Tate waving at me a few tables away.

"Harp, over here." Tate stood and pulled out a chair for me, something he hadn't done since the early days of our dating when we were still in college.

I slid into the seat across from him, trying not to let my nerves show on my face as I put my phone on the table. "Merry Christmas, Tate."

"Merry Christmas." He smiled at me and slid a small package across the table, giving me a strange sense of déjà vu of past Christmases spent together. "I got you something."

"You shouldn't have." I didn't move to open it, but judging by its rectangular shape, it was a book. Which made sense. That was what we'd gotten each other both Christmases when we'd dated.

He smiled and it transformed his face from that of a closet poet to a class jokester. His strong jawline and high cheekbones meshed with his smattering of freckles to make him look young and innocent—something I'd fallen for the first time.

"Tate, I didn't ask you to come here because I'm willing to give you another chance."

"You didn't?" His jaw worked as if he was fighting for more words.

"No." I shook my head. "I asked you to come because I know you needed to talk to me, and I also wanted to talk to you."

He leaned back in his chair and folded his arms.

"I wanted to say that I forgive you." That was true, at least.

He straightened at that, blinking in surprise. "You do?"

"Yes." I smiled at Nancy as she dropped off a caramel cocoa for me before I ordered. It was nice to be where people knew what you loved.

"I didn't think you ever would," he said softly.

"I know. I didn't think I would either." I gave him a small smile. "But if it hadn't been for you, I might not have come to Whisper Hollow. And as hard as everything was, this is where I'm meant to be. If I'd married you, I would've missed out on my whole life here."

He frowned. "Maybe I should have gone first …"

"Why?"

"Because I still think we can be together, Harp. I'm sorry for what I did, but we can make this work." He gave me a hopeful smile, lifting his eyebrows slightly.

I sighed. Why had I never realized what a terrible listener he was? "I don't want to keep having this conversation anymore, Tate, and I don't want to make a relationship with you work. I don't even want you calling me Harp anymore. We're over."

"But I can't give up." He fidgeted in his seat, not meeting my gaze. "I need you. And if you want to stay here, I can stay here too. We can run your grandmother's shop together. I could—"

"Tate, why are you here?"

He scratched at his arm—a sure sign of his nerves. "Because I missed you."

"Try again." I shook my head. "I saw you talking to Helen the other day. I know you know her."

He flinched. "Okay, maybe I haven't been entirely honest."

"You think?" I gave him a hard stare. That was nothing new. "What's going on with Helen?"

"Nothing. She's just a friend of a friend, but that doesn't matter." He spread his fingers out on the table and leaned toward me. "I need your help. I've been wanting to talk to you for days, and I even waited for you outside your shop."

"I never saw you." I edged back in my seat but didn't look at Seb to avoid giving his presence away. Just having him there was enough.

"I couldn't wait right in front. I was worried someone would see me so I waited in the alley."

"Who would see you?" The rest of his words caught up to me. "Wait, that was you in the alley?" It was Tate we'd passed in the alley that night—Tate who Helen said she'd seen?

My stomach dropped to my toes as the pieces clicked into place. The anxious behavior. The cigarette wrappers outside my house and the shop. Him lying to me again and again.

Had I been wrong about it not being his brand of cigarettes?

"Did you start smoking again, Tate?"

His finger twitched on the table. "What? No, of course not. I quit, you know that. And I only waited in the alley the one time. I'm not a stalker."

His answer would be more believable if he wasn't acting jumpy like he had when he'd first quit smoking.

"Why have you been following me?" I tried to keep my voice steady.

"I've been waiting for a time to talk to you alone," he continued, almost muttering now. "You're always with someone."

His lack of denial washed over me like a chill draft sneaking through the window. Oh, crap. Seb was right. Tate *was* the one who'd been following me around. Which meant that he was at the top of the suspect list for Tom's murder. The police had already said the person following me was most likely the killer.

Could Tate be the murderer? There was an edge to his narrowed eyes that I hadn't noticed before, like our time apart had hardened him, turned him into someone I didn't recognize, someone far from the man I had once hoped to marry. Maybe I never really knew Tate after all.

I leaned back to put more distance between us. "I'm not comfortable meeting with you alone, Tate. There's a killer on the loose. If you want to talk, now is your chance."

He blanched and scratched his arm again, leaning close and lowering his voice. "That's what I need to talk to you about."

As casually as I could despite my racing pulse, I tapped my phone in the agreed-upon signal. From the corner of my eye, I saw Seb get up and walk around the counter to talk to Nancy, then her gaze darted my way as if she could see the danger looming over me like a dark cloud. Thankfully, Tate's back was to them, so he saw none of it.

"I'm in trouble, Harp. I need your help." Tate's expression flickered with a mixture of desperation and determination.

"Need *my* help? Why?" My voice rose as the rapid thudding of my heart echoed my rising panic.

"Promise me you won't tell anyone. I could get in serious trouble."

Was that a confession? I fought to breathe normally while the bakery seemed to close in around me. How could I have almost married someone capable of this? Had I ever truly been safe when I was with him?

"Are you the reason Tom's dead?" My words came out as a whisper.

"It's not what you think." Guilt and terror flashed across his features. "I know I should talk to the police, but it's too risky."

His guilt, more than anything else, hit me like a slap of cold water.

The soft murmur of conversation and the clinking of utensils created a facade of normalcy that contrasted sharply with my growing dread. "How could you hurt Tom? You didn't even know him." I couldn't stop the accusation lacing my voice, but I tried to tone it down in case Tate had a gun on him. Hadn't Sheriff Warner said that was how Tom died?

"I didn't mean for him to get mixed up in this. That's why I've been so desperate to track you down. I'm in danger." Tate's eyes pleaded for understanding.

I gasped as the weight of his words sank in. He wasn't denying it.

"We still have a chance. There's nothing I can do about Tom, but you can still help me." His voice trembled and he tried to put a hand on mine across the table, but I shrank from the contact. "If you ever cared about me, please just give me some money, I can fix everything. I can make it all go away."

I blinked, struggling to process everything, and my gaze locked on his face, searching for any remnants of the person I used to love. "Money?"

Tate flushed. "I didn't want to have to tell you this, but yes. I need some money."

The conversations around me grew muted and distorted, and I put my head in my hands. My entire body shook, and while I wanted to run away, I wasn't sure I could move. I couldn't believe Tate killed Tom. And over money. If I'd thought he'd broken my heart and shattered my trust before, it was nothing compared to how I felt now. My insides felt like the ice Seb scraped off my windshield—cold and brittle and like someone had just hollowed me out.

"I promise that if you give me money, I can leave your life forever if that's what you want." Tate stood and reached for my shoulder. "Please, Harp."

The contact snapped me back to reality, and I jolted from his touch. Every instinct in me screamed to get up and run, but I couldn't endanger the rest of the people in the bakery.

As if in answer to my plea, the front doors burst open. Tate's eyes widened as officers streamed into the bakery.

Tate looked around. "What's going on?"

"Tate Harris," Sheriff Warner said, "you're under arrest for the murder of Tom Stevens."

"What?" His eyes widened. "No, it wasn't me."

Sheriff Warner shoved Tate down against the table, then handcuffed his hands behind his back. Tate's cup of coffee fell to the floor and shattered with a tinkling crash, spilling the dark liquid everywhere.

I sucked in a breath. The pooling dark liquid curved around Tate's feet like the blood around Mr. James's body.

"Harp, tell them I'm innocent!" Tate cried.

I stood and stumbled away from the table.

Seb appeared at my side and wrapped me in his arms. "It's okay," he murmured into my hair. "I'm here."

It was then I realized I was trembling. I rested my forehead against his chest, soaking in his warmth. His comfort.

The police escorted Tate from the building, but he continued to yell things like, "Wait! Please. It wasn't me. Harp, help!"

His cries faded into the distance as the doors closed. I stared out the glass display window as Tate was loaded into the back of a police car while a few officers came back in to reassure the customers.

Sheriff Warner walked over to Seb and me. "Thanks for your call. We've been searching for him all morning."

"Thanks for responding so quickly." Seb's deep voice rumbled against my ear with my head pressed against his chest.

"Wait." I pulled back from Seb and looked at both men. "What do you mean you've been searching for him?"

"Yeah"—Sheriff Warner looked between Seb and me—"That lighter we found at the scene of the crime had quite a few fingerprints on it, but we couldn't find a match in the system until Sebastian sent in the ornament and told us who'd touched it. Once we had the two to compare, the rest was just a matter of tracking him down."

"What ornament?" I asked.

"The glass book ornament thing," Sheriff Warner said.

Seb frowned and turned to me. "Sorry I didn't mention it. You seemed so against the idea of even suspecting Tate that I thought I should do it on my own. And after Tate touched that thing in your store, I wanted to act before his fingerprints disappeared."

So that's why Seb had seemed like he was hiding something the other night. I'd thought it was strange for the ornament to suddenly go missing, but I'd never suspected Seb of taking it. He'd sent it off without telling me, even though we were supposed to be working as a team.

The betrayal stung, even if he'd done it for my protection.

Was there no one I could trust not to lie to me?

Chapter 15

Naughty or Nice

"What does that mean for Helen?" I forced my mind back to the problem at hand, and not Seb's betrayal. Did one little white lie even matter when he'd been doing it to help me?

Sheriff Warner's forehead crinkled in a frown. "What do you mean?"

I gripped Seb's hand tightly and turned to the sheriff. "We think they were working together."

Behind the counter, the officer who had been there when we'd found the murder weapon under the bookshelf in Whispering Pages was talking to Nancy.

"We didn't catch all the details, but we overheard them talking about something at the Christmas festival." Seb explained the few things we'd gleaned from their conversation while the sheriff's expression grew grimmer.

"We can help," I said abruptly. "Maybe Seb can get her to confess."

"We took her off our suspect list fairly early in the investigation, but maybe we'll bring her in for more questions once we're done talking to Mr. Harris." Sheriff Warner pulled on his mustache. "But you two don't need to be involved anymore. You should go home and enjoy your Christmas."

The car holding Tate finally pulled from the lot and into the street, but watching him disappear fueled my determination to make sure Helen didn't get away.

"I understand, Sheriff." I tugged Seb away to run my idea by him, but I was intercepted by Nancy.

She pulled me into a hug. "Oh my goodness, are you all right?"

"I'm okay." But I didn't feel okay. Tate had just been taken away for murder and I'd found out that Seb had lied to me.

Despite my reassurance, she kept patting my back and my arm as if making sure I was whole. "I was so worried about you when Seb told me what was going on."

"I'm sorry to have scared you," I said. "But everything is all right now." Or at least it would be once we talked to Helen. Whatever Sheriff Warner said, we had to finish this. We were missing the final piece of the puzzle, but once we had it, I could finally put all this behind me.

My heart twinged as I realized that also meant I'd be putting Seb behind me too. Maybe we could go back to our dinners at Nancy's together, but nothing would be the same now that I realized my feelings for him.

"You sure know how to pick them." Nancy tsked and shook her head.

"Nancy," I hissed with a concerned look at Seb.

"Oh, I'm sorry. I didn't mean it like that."

He stiffened. "It's okay."

The thought of losing Seb made me realize his lie didn't matter after all. Unlike Tate's lies, Seb had only ever wanted to protect me, and if

I asked him not to hide the truth from me again, I was sure he would agree.

Nancy looked at us. "Are you sure you two want to talk to Helen now? It isn't too late to go home and enjoy the rest of your Christmas together."

"This is something we have to do," I said firmly. In a way, as the one who'd inadvertently brought Tate to town and caused Tom's death, I felt like I had to see it through. Even now it was still hard to believe that Tate was truly involved. Maybe Helen had somehow put him up to it.

"All right, but don't let Leo catch wind of your plans." Nancy hugged me again and bustled off.

As much as I wanted to wrap up this case, at the same time, I couldn't help wishing I could drag it out a little longer so I could have more time with Seb. Having him around made everything better. I needed his humor in my life, the way the smallest touch of his hand made my heart flutter, the feeling of truly being seen when he looked at me.

"How are we going to do this?" I asked Seb as we stepped outside.

"We can swing by her place and ask her." He lowered his voice since a few townspeople were still nearby, buzzing with chatter about the arrest.

"I don't think she'll talk to you if I'm there," I said. "It needs to be somewhere I can hide."

Which was how I found myself bundled in two layers of coats and hiding behind a copse of trees at Serenity Park, while Seb sat in the gazebo waiting for Helen. A fresh blanket of snow from last night had transformed the park into a serene winter wonderland and covered up the many footprints and tracks from the night of the festival.

The trees stood tall and proud, their bare branches adorned with delicate icicles that glimmered in the sunlight. Silver and white painted our surroundings as if the world had been dipped in a shimmering, frosty charm. If it had been any other Christmas morning, it would've felt magical.

"Do you think she'll come?" I said into my cell phone. My breath hung in the air in a wispy cloud before dissipating into the clear blue sky above.

"I think so," Seb's low voice answered, and he shifted on the bench.

I shifted in place, and the patch of snow under me crunched softly. A group of snowmen with carrot noses and cheerful pebble grins stood near the playground, leering at me as if they knew something I didn't.

"I hope she comes soon." I held my hands in front of my mouth and breathed on them.

"She's here." Seb put his phone in his pocket but left it connected on speakerphone so I could hear.

Helen, wearing a soft-knit sweater dress and warm woolen tights under a dark pea coat, walked up the steps to the gazebo and sat by Seb. "Hey, Seb, I'm glad you called."

If I strained, I could hear her speak even without the phone, so I hung up. It was safer that way.

"I'm glad you came," Seb said.

"I'll admit, I was surprised to hear from you." Helen put a hand on his arm, giving him a coy smile. "But it was a pleasant surprise."

Seb didn't shift away from her touch, and I ground my teeth.

"I wanted to talk to you alone." Seb turned so their knees were touching.

"Does this mean you've ended things with that woman?"

I scowled at her. The way she called me "that woman" made it sound like *I* was trying to steal *her* man. The thought brought me up short as I had to remind myself once again that Seb wasn't really mine.

"No, I haven't," Seb said.

Helen's hand slid up his arm, and she scooted closer. "That's okay. I can be flexible."

Seb caught her hand and held it. "Actually, that's why I wanted to talk to you. I know you were talking to Tate."

Helen stiffened but then gave him a small smile. "Oh, so you know about that?"

My breath caught. She'd finally admitted it. Seb just needed to push a little more and get a confession.

"He told Harp," Seb said.

Helen scowled and flipped her hair over her shoulder. "I should've known better than to trust him."

"He isn't the most reliable guy," Seb said stiffly.

"Well, regardless, if you're interested in me, I don't need him anymore." Helen flashed him another coy smile that I could read even from where I hid, then leaned forward with her eyes closed.

My heart took off. She was going to kiss him.

Seb grabbed her arm, stopping her. "I'm not interested in dating you. I'm dating Harper."

Helen's eyes flew open, then narrowed in a scowl. "What do you even see in her, anyway? Do you love her or something?"

Seb hesitated, and I chewed on my lower lip. He probably had no idea how far he'd have to take this fake dating scenario when he first agreed to it.

"I do," Seb said clearly. "I love Harper."

My breath caught, and for a moment, the world froze around me. *I love Harper.*

"But why? You and I could work so well," Helen said. "I've known it since the moment you stood up for me when Tom and I had that fight."

"I'm sorry. I don't see you like that." Seb was ever the gentleman, even when he was talking to a potential killer's accomplice.

"If you tell me what you love about her, I can change. I could be that way too."

"You can't be like Harp." Seb shook his head. "No one can. She's fierce and kind and thoughtful and brave."

My heart threatened to pound its way free of my chest.

Seb stopped and cleared his throat. "And most of all, she would never do what you've done."

Seb's next words brought me crashing back to reality. He was following a script and trying to get her to confess when I was over here getting excited like an idiot. What was I thinking? Seb was still playing a part.

"I only did what was necessary to go after what I wanted," Helen said. "After all, isn't that what everyone does?"

"So, you admit that you had something to do with Tom's murder?" Seb asked.

"What? Of course not." Helen leaned back. "That's crazy. Why would you think that?"

"I heard you and Tate talking about it at the Christmas Festival, Helen."

She shook her head, and her long curls bounced around her shoulders. "No, we didn't."

"There's no point lying." Seb's voice hardened. "I heard you. You mentioned making sure no one found out what you two did."

Her cheeks matched her red dress. "That wasn't what we were talking about."

"You can't hide it." Seb folded his arms. "Tate is already under arrest for Tom's murder."

"Tate killed Tom?" Her eyes widened. "Is this about the gambling?"

Did Tom have a gambling issue? Did that have something to do with Tate's money issues?

"It's too late to act innocent."

"I swear that I had no idea," she cried. "I'd never hurt Tom like that."

"You just hurt him emotionally by cheating on him, is that it?"

She flushed again. "I didn't say I was perfect, but that doesn't make me guilty of murder."

"Then tell me what you and Tate were talking about."

If this wasn't about Tom's murder, what was it about? The moment dragged on, and I chewed on my thumbnail. I should have reminded Seb to ask Helen *how* she and Tate even knew each other.

Helen's gaze darted around as if making sure they were alone. It was a good thing I was hiding, because I had a feeling she never would've admitted any of this if I had been there.

"We were planning how to break you and Harper up." She wouldn't meet his gaze now. "Tate mentioned he was desperate to get back with Harp, and I wasn't ... opposed to the idea of dating you, so we thought we could help each other out. Tom and I had been having some trouble, and it seemed like a good idea."

I blinked at her profile. This whole time, it had been about dating. All their secrets and lies were because they were trying to get Seb and I to break up. She'd just lost her boyfriend, and she was already scheming how to take someone else's. I could almost laugh at the absurdity of the situation, since we weren't really dating to begin with. I'd thought María was ridiculous, but she'd been right after all.

"I swear I had no idea he was the murderer." She shivered and crossed her arms.

"So, you didn't have anything to do with Tom's death?" Seb said slowly.

"No," she said. "I know I don't have an alibi for the night he was killed, but I do have proof that I'm telling the truth. One of my friends knew about our plan to break you two up the whole time. She could vouch for me."

If Tate was in custody and Helen had nothing to do with the murder, then that meant the case was officially over.

Instead of being elated, my heart sank. There was no longer any reason for Seb and me to keep dating.

It was time to stop pretending.

Chapter 16

Silent Night, Deadly Night

"Well, I guess we were wrong about her after all," Seb said to me once Helen was gone.

His words were meant to be comforting, but they only served as a painful reminder of a truth I couldn't avoid any longer. Helen was innocent, Tate had been arrested, and the charade we'd been living was unraveling.

"I'm glad we got things straightened out." Seb's fingers found mine, his touch warm yet distant, a silent acknowledgment of the inevitable. His tight grip said, "This is the end," and my heart clenched in response.

"Me too."

We made our way to the car, each step pulling at me. I didn't want to face the truth. I didn't want to tell Seb it was over, that our time together had come to an end. But I couldn't prolong it anymore.

"You okay?" Seb asked as we buckled our seat belts. "You're pretty quiet."

"It's just ... been a lot." At least that was true, although going to confront Tate this morning felt significantly less risky than the conversation with Seb looming over me. The weight of it pressed down on me, a heaviness that threatened to suffocate my already aching heart.

"True." Seb sighed and started the car, then turned the heater on full blast. "It's been a heck of a morning. Should we go home?"

Home? He said it so casually, even now living his role. I turned and stared out the window. "Yeah, I guess we should." The conversation could at least wait until we were home, so we weren't trapped in the car.

We spent the next few minutes in silence while I stared out the window. A few people were out and about, wearing cozy scarves and mittens, their faces rosy and their breath visible in the chilly air as they hurried to their destinations, but otherwise, the town was silent. The cheerful lights and vibrant decorations mocked the heaviness in my chest.

As we idled at a stoplight at the edge of town, I peered through the frosty front window of a cheerfully decorated house and watched a family exchanging presents around a Christmas tree. The sight pricked at my heart like shards of glass. That's how I thought today would go for Seb and me, but reality had a cruel way of tearing fantasies apart.

I couldn't drag this out any longer. The kisses. The soft touches. His fake confession to Helen. All of it was too hard to endure when my feelings were so painfully apparent.

"It's hard to believe it's over," Seb said as we pulled into my driveway.

I jolted in my seat. "Over?" The finality in his voice twisted my heart with fresh pain, even though I'd been mentally preparing myself.

The car's engine hummed consolingly as my world fell apart.

"Yeah, the murder case." He glanced at me, then unbuckled. "I know it's been less than a week, but it sure feels like it's been hanging over us a lot longer than that. Now we can finally stop worrying."

"And stop pretending," I said, my voice barely above a whisper, the words catching in my throat.

"What?" He stiffened.

"Now that you no longer need an alibi and Tate isn't chasing after me anymore, you don't have to pretend to be my boyfriend anymore." As much as I wanted to delay the inevitable, the words tumbled out, each syllable laden with heartbreak.

He turned to me, his gaze piercing. A myriad of emotions flickered in their blue depths. "Is that what you want?"

I bit my lip as memories of Seb flashed through my mind. Seb and I roasting marshmallows by the fire. Seb kissing me under the mistletoe. Seb telling Helen he loved me. I wanted it to be real so badly that I ached for it. But I couldn't tell him that. He'd offered to help me because he cared about me as a friend, and I couldn't risk our friendship by pressuring him with expectations. He'd told me at the beginning how important my friendship was to him, and I couldn't repay his kindness like that.

My throat closed up and tears pricked at my eyes, threatening to spill over and shatter my fragile control. "Yes." I couldn't bear the thought of ending what we had, but I couldn't bear the thought of living a lie even more or the thought of him apologizing for everything we'd shared in our fake relationship the same way he'd apologized for kissing me.

We sat in the car, an invisible thread tying us together and simultaneously pulling us apart.

"Well, if you're sure." Seb unbuckled his seatbelt, his movements slow and deliberate, as if he was trying to prolong our final moments with each other.

"Thanks for everything until now." I didn't want him to feel like he had to keep doing me any favors. "You don't have to stay here anymore. I'm sure you're anxious to get back to staying at a place free of cat hairs." I tried to inject some playfulness into my tone, but based on the serious look he was giving me, he probably didn't buy it.

He smiled but it didn't reach his eyes. "It isn't so bad as long as I remember to take my pills."

We sat for a moment, neither of us moving or saying anything. The seconds ticked away, stealing what time we had left.

"Do you really want me to go?" he said after a painfully long pause.

No, of course not. Having you with me has been the most fun I've had in a long time.

I swallowed the words back, my throat closing up with unshed tears. If only he hadn't apologized for kissing me—both times. The one in public *maybe* I could understand. What if he'd felt bad for putting on a show? But why apologize for kissing me at my house? And why had I thought that someone might like me for real after Tate had proven how fickle feelings could be? "It's for the best."

Stiffly, he got out of the car. "I should go. I'll come for my stuff later."

"Okay," I whispered, my heart shattering all over again.

This was officially the worst Christmas ever.

Despite everything, he waited until I was inside my house before driving away.

I called Grace as soon as Seb's car disappeared.

"Merry Christmas," she said after picking up.

"Merry—" I started sobbing. Her voice unlocked the grief I'd barely restrained throughout my conversation with Seb.

"Harp?" Her voice edged with panic. "What's wrong?"

I couldn't answer her for a minute as my sobs intensified, but eventually, they slowed a bit until I was just hiccuping. "I ... ended things with Seb." My voice broke on every syllable but somehow, I made it through the sentence.

"Oh, Harp. I'm sorry," she said. "I wish I could be there with you."

"At least I'm heading your way in a few days."

"A few days feels like an eternity when your baby sister is crying on the phone and you can't do anything to help."

I sniffed and wiped my running nose, letting the tree's cheerful glow lead me down the hall. "I'll be okay," I said. "Eventually."

"I know you will."

"I knew this would hurt. This was why I didn't want to put myself out there again." I stopped in the living room and stared at the spot where Seb and I had slept last night. He'd rolled up the sleeping bags this morning because he didn't want me to worry about it. He was always doing thoughtful things like that.

"Now, Harp, that's not fair. Seb didn't hurt you; you hurt yourself."

I pinched my eyes shut, though that did little to stop Grace's lecture. "Can't you just let me wallow in peace?"

"Maybe if I thought it was good for you," she said. "But did you give Sebastian a chance?"

"What do you mean?" I collapsed on the couch and leaned my head back, staring at the ceiling. Without Seb around, the house felt large and empty.

"Well, what did you tell him when you broke up with him?"

"That he didn't need to keep pretending anymore since the police arrested Tate for Tom's murder this morning."

"What?" she screeched through the phone. "I can't believe"—she stopped and exhaled slowly—"actually, we'll get back to that later. I have a lot to say, but I feel like we should focus on Sebastian right now. What did he say after you told him that?"

"He asked if that was what I really wanted."

"And?"

"And I told him that it was."

A faint slapping sound came from the other end, as if Grace had hit her forehead with her palm. "Why did you say that?"

My stomach twisted, and more tears pricked at my eyes. "Because I'm tired of pretending."

Grace was quiet for a moment, and the silence gave me a chance to hear frustrated meowing coming from upstairs. I climbed back to my feet with a sigh to check on Jiji, trying not to look at the fireplace where Seb and I had cooked marshmallows just last night.

"It sounds like you've fallen for Sebastian for real," she said softly.

"I did," I finally admitted it to her but to her credit, she didn't say, "I told you so."

"Then why didn't you tell him that?"

"I don't want him to feel pressured to date me. It isn't fair to him. And we kissed last night, but then he apologized for it, just like he did when we kissed at the festival." I made my way up the stairs, following the sound of Jiji's cries. Almost immediately, I saw the problem. The doors upstairs were closed, even though I usually left them open since Jiji hated closed doors. Seb must've forgotten and accidentally shut her in his room that morning.

"Did you ask him why he apologized?"

"Are you kidding? It was embarrassing enough as it is."

"Sometimes relationships require being a little vulnerable, Harp," she said. "If there's one thing I've learned from being married, it's that none of us are mind readers and it isn't fair to expect someone to be. You need open communication."

I flushed and pushed open my bedroom door. Jiji darted out with an angry hiss and turned and kept meowing.

"Why is this all on me?" I said as I continued down the hall to Seb's room. "If he was interested in dating for real, he could've said something."

"True." She was silent for a moment. "And I'm not saying for sure that Seb wants to date you, and I don't know why he apologized for kissing you, but think of it from his perspective. You were the one who suddenly said you wanted to go back to being friends. He was probably surprised."

Now that she pointed it out, he had seemed surprised. Stunned even.

"And him asking you if that's what you wanted sort of feels like a good sign to me."

Some of the broken pieces in my heart tried to slide back together. I walked through the guest room, taking in the few items Seb had left behind. A small bag hanging from the back of the chair by the desk. A book sitting on the nightstand by the bed. The floor creaked as I made my way over to examine the stub of paper poking out of the book. It was the ticket stub from our not-date on the ice rink.

"Do you really think there's hope?" I put the phone on speaker and laid it next to me as I snuggled on Seb's carefully made bed. Jiji still meowed at me from the doorway, her fur standing on end angrily. Why was she still freaking out?

"There's always hope," Grace said.

Spoken like one who got married young.

"Should I say something to him?" The thought had my heart racing.

"I'm not going to tell you what to do, Harp. You need to decide this one on your own."

"I'm scared," I whispered.

"I know," she said. "But since you're already hurting now, think of it this way. What would you regret more: telling or not telling him how you feel?"

Her words echoed Loren's from that morning. He'd been brave enough to take his shot and ask me out, but when it was my turn to put my heart on the line for Seb, I'd run away.

I blew out a breath and climbed to my feet. "You're right. I was an idiot to let him go. I'm going to find him." Maybe I would regret confessing to Seb, but it couldn't be any worse than how I felt now. I was an idiot for letting fear rule me. Seb was nothing like Tate. I could trust him. And even if he didn't want to date me, I could still trust him to take care of me as a friend.

"Good for you."

In the hall, I stooped to pet Jiji and tried to calm her, but she hissed again and darted away.

"Was that Jiji? What's wrong with her?" Grace asked.

"I don't know. She's been freaking out since I got home." I straightened and started down the hall to go back downstairs.

The floor in Seb's room creaked behind me, and I froze.

That spot only creaked when someone stepped on it.

A shiver raced down my back.

I looked over my shoulder and found a tall figure in black standing several steps behind me in the hall. A mask hid most of the man's face, but the unmistakable shape of a gun was tucked into his belt.

A scream burst from me, and I raced down the stairs. "Grace, call the police. There's someone—"

A hand covered my mouth and yanked me back, and my phone clattered to the floor.

"Harp? What's going on?" Panic surged through Grace's voice, matching the terror flowing through me.

I struggled to fight the man off, but a sweet, cloying odor slipped into my nose and my body grew heavy.

"Harper, answer me!"

I tried, but the overwhelming odor dragged me into darkness.

Chapter 17

Run Rudolph Run

A pounding headache woke me, and my stomach curled with nausea. Slowly, I inhaled through my nose and exhaled through my mouth. The cold air was thick with a damp, musty smell, as if I was sitting in an old shoe locker, and cold, hard concrete chilled my cheek.

I opened my eyes, but the darkness didn't go away. Instead, it pressed in from all sides, swallowing me whole. My heart beat faster, and my breathing turned erratic. My arms were tied together in front of me and something tight cinched around my ankles. A shiver raced through me.

Where was I?

Panic shot through my veins as fragmented memories flooded my mind, piecing together the horrifying truth: I had been kidnapped.

A shudder ripped through me while my mind raced. Who was he? Why had he taken me? The panicked questions swirled in my mind like splashes of color, mixing until they were nothing more than a sense of crushing black.

I'd been talking to Grace when I'd been taken, and she'd known something was wrong. But even if the police came to my house, what would they find there? My phone on the ground and a furious Jiji?

I couldn't wait around for someone to find me, and there was no guarantee help was coming, even if I did. I needed to figure out a way out of this myself. I had to calm down.

With a grunt, I tried to move, but my body was heavy. Possibly another side effect of whatever drug that man had used on me. My shoes were gone, though thankfully I still had socks. The rough fibers of the rope cut into the bare skin of my wrists, except for the area covered by my bracelet.

My bracelet! I'd been an idiot for not using the pepper spray the first time, but terror had overcome my logic. If I could just get my hands free, maybe I could use it on him and escape. I had no idea where I was, but anything was better than being locked up in this room.

Slowly, my eyes adjusted to the gloom until I could make out the outline of a scraggly Christmas tree in the corner and a wreath leaning against the wall. Was I in a storage room?

This was now *officially* the worst Christmas ever.

In the distance, a faint creak echoed, followed by the sound of muffled footsteps and the click of a switch. Light spilled through the crack under the door.

My pulse took off in response.

Someone was coming.

The clank of a key in a lock sounded, then another door opened with a sluggish groan. This one brought a flood of light into the gloom. I squinted at the sudden brightness.

A shadowy figure stood in the doorway, illuminated by the light behind him.

Fear rooted me to my spot on the ground. Instinctively, I prayed he wouldn't notice me, though it was obvious he'd come just to see me.

He took a step forward, leaving the brightness behind, but then the room's murky darkness obscured his features just as much. His approach brought the acrid smell of smoke into the room.

"You're awake, I see." His soft tenor was familiar, but I couldn't place it immediately. It sounded more like the voice of a jolly old man dressed up as Santa Claus than the voice of a kidnapper, but the harsh reality around me said otherwise.

"What do you want?" My voice quivered as I fought for some shred of bravery among the terror flowing through me.

"I want my money."

Money? My mind raced to keep up. "What money?"

"The money that's owed to me."

Hadn't Tate said something about needing money? Was this the man he'd owed it to? Or maybe this had something to do with Tom's gambling issues Helen had mentioned.

The man took another step, and I could finally see more of his face. It was Walter—the man from the bookstore. The bakery. The Christmas Festival. He'd been following me all along, and I'd never suspected a thing.

"I need your help convincing our friend Tate to give me the money he owes before anyone else gets hurt. He's been difficult to deal with lately." Walter pulled out a pack of cigarettes from his pocket, and even in the dim lighting, I could make out the stripe of blue around the box.

I froze, putting the final pieces of the puzzle together. It was Walter who'd been following me, him who'd left those footprints outside my house and the wrapper next to my car. Tate had been telling the truth. Maybe he'd been in the alley that one time, but all the other times it had been Walter. He'd come for Tate, which would explain who Tate had been hiding from, and somehow Tom must've gotten mixed up in it too.

"Why me?" I whispered.

"I went through Tate's house after he left to figure out where he might've gone, and I followed him here. You and Tom were two of the first people he sought out after arriving."

That must've been when he got the lighter from Tate's house.

"Why kill Tom if it's Tate you're after?" I fought to keep my voice steady.

"You figured that out, huh?" He smirked, his bushy eyebrows pulling into a leer. "Tate wasn't the only one who owed me money."

"What do you expect me to do?" I tried to keep my breathing slow and even to keep from hyperventilating.

"Now that I have you, I think Tate will finally pay up." He pulled out a cell phone. "You're going to call and tell him exactly what I have written."

The shiver was back, violently racing down my back. Didn't Walter realize Tate was in jail?

I swallowed and bit my lip. Of course not. He'd probably already been lying in wait at my place when Tate was arrested that morning. But what other choice did I have? If I told him Tate was in jail, he might get violent. "Okay."

"I mean *exactly*," he said. "Otherwise"—he lifted his shirt, revealing the gun tucked into his pants—"it'll be a short conversation."

"Okay." I fought to keep my voice steady and wiggled my fingers to keep the blood flowing. Whether I did what he said or not, my chances of getting out alive weren't looking good. Now that I'd seen his face, what are the odds he'd let me live?

I didn't dare touch my bracelet, in case it drew his attention, but the pepper spray on my wrist was a comforting weight.

Walter pushed the door open wider, letting in more light, then pulled out a notebook and angled it for me to read. He punched a number into his phone and put it on speaker.

My pounding heart somewhat muted the phone's shrill ring. If Tate was still with the police, where would his phone be?

It rang again.

That was a good sign. At least it was turned on. Hopefully.

Another ring.

I stared at the phone, avoiding Walter's searing gaze.

What would happen to me if nobody answered?

It rang again.

"Harper, is that you?" Tate exhaled loudly. "I thought something was wrong. Grace called the police freaking out, and—"

Relief rushed through me as it connected. "Hi."

Walter touched the notebook and scowled.

I squinted at the short, blocky writing. "You've taken too long, and someone already died." My heart gave a pang as I thought of Tom. "If you want to see me alive again, pay what you owe."

"Harp, what are you saying? Where are you?"

"Follow the directions in the text and keep the police out of this." My stomach tightened with nerves. If Walter realized Tate was with the police right then, what would he do to me?

"Tell me where you ar—"

Walter snatched the phone back and disconnected it, leaving silence ringing between us.

We stared at each other, the moment stretched taut between us. "If your boyfriend doesn't pay up, *you* will." He slammed the door closed behind him and locked it, leaving me in darkness again.

Once I was alone, I let out a shuddering breath, then got to work picking at the ropes around my wrist with my teeth. I was losing feeling in my toes, but my fingers felt a little better. I must've loosened the knot.

The cords resisted my efforts at first, gnawing into my skin every time I moved. Ignoring the burning pain, I kept at it, although I had to stop frequently to spit out the coarse fibers. Dirt and dust coated my tongue, drying out my mouth, but I persisted.

After a while, my jaw ached from the effort, and beads of sweat trickled down my forehead. My hands had lost feeling a while ago, from the tightness of the knot, the cold, and having to hold them up for so long.

Minutes turned into what felt like hours as I continued painstakingly picking at my bonds. I couldn't help but glance toward the door every few seconds. Walter could come back at any moment.

The ropes loosened a bit, and a surge of hope propelled me to attack the knot again with renewed vigor.

Something creaked outside, and panic rushed through me like a flash of lightning.

I had to get out.

With one final tug from my teeth, I slipped one hand free and sucked in a breath as the cold air met the raw skin. I quickly disentangled my other hand.

Relief and adrenaline flooded through me as I stood up. My legs protested the sudden movement, and I leaned against the wall for support.

Now what?

I tried the door, but it was, of course, locked. I hadn't expected otherwise, but I would've been an idiot not to try. I looked around, but there were no windows, and the only vent was too small to fit through. My only chance to get out of here would be when Walter came back.

I'd have to surprise him and then make a run for it. Hopefully, there weren't any cameras hidden in the room.

The thought sent my heart racing, but I welcomed the feeling as long as it didn't make me freeze. But no, I'd made that mistake earlier and refused to do it again. I touched the bracelet on my wrist, reassuring myself that it was still there.

My whole body trembled with exhaustion—or maybe it was nerves. I shook out my arms and stretched my legs, trying to loosen them up and make sure they weren't asleep. I had to be ready. I shifted my weight from foot to foot. If only I had a pair of shoes to protect my feet.

Every creak from the house around me set me on edge. The noises seemed to echo in the otherwise silent room.

After what seemed like an eternity, the heavy thump of the man's footsteps sounded in the hall again.

It was time.

My pulse skyrocketed as I tried to remember whether the door opened in or out. Where should I stand? Should I pretend like I was still tied up and then surprise him once he got close? No, then I'd just waste valuable time having to get to the door. I'd wait next to it, so I'd be ready to run. My captor's eyes should take a moment to adjust to the room's darkness, which would give me the time I needed to spray him.

The footsteps grew louder, their thumping making me think he was going down a set of stairs. I must've been in a basement.

Every part of my body tightened in anticipation as the click of the lock sounded again.

I breathed out once slowly, trying to steady my shaking hands as I held them in the air, one hand over the bracelet, ready to spray.

In what seemed like slow motion, the door opened, flooding the room with light again.

"Time to—"

I held my breath and aimed directly at his eyes, then closed mine and sprayed.

Walter swore, and I could hear him moving around.

I cracked my eyes open, and even that caused them to sting from the spray. But I didn't hesitate to slip through the narrow space beside him.

His arm flailed in the air, and his fingers closed around my wrist like a vice.

My breath caught in my chest, but I spun around and rotated my wrist to loosen his grip, then I kicked him between his legs.

He released me with a string of swears.

Heart pounding, I ran up the stairs in the stark light of a naked bulb in the ceiling. The musty scent of old wood hung in the air. Fear propelled me forward, my feet slapping against the wooden steps with desperate urgency.

Walter swore again and his fumbling footsteps chased after me, but I dared not look back. "You're going to regret this." The sharp explosion of a gun sounded behind me.

I threw my hands over my head but didn't let myself stop even though my ears were ringing. The bullet hit the wall, flinging sheetrock at my arm.

I ducked and kept moving, grateful his vision was impaired. Adrenaline coursed through my veins, urging me to run faster. I made it to the top of the stairs and burst into a living room. Ignoring the stockings hanging by the fireplace and the family photos lining the walls, I spun around to lock it, but it was one of those old ones that required a key. I swore and bolted for the exit, pushing through the burn in my legs and the ache in my lungs. My trembling hands fumbled with the knob to the front door, my fingers slipping in my haste.

Behind me, the sound of stumbling footsteps and heavy breathing grew nearer.

I gripped the cool metal and twisted it desperately, praying it would open.

Once it burst open, I stumbled into the night's inky darkness. Was it still the same day I'd been taken, or was Christmas over? The cold air hit me with a slap, and I shivered as I ran down the porch. Gravel and snow crunched under my socks as I sprinted across the driveway, eyes fixed on a distant line of trees. I ignored the pain in my feet and forced myself to move faster.

Moonlight flickered through the branches overhead, casting eerie shadows on the ground. They should have frightened me, but I rushed into their embrace, wanting nothing more than to lose myself in their gloom so Walter couldn't find me again.

I was so close to being free.

The distant sound of my captor's pursuit chased me into the trees. A twig snapped under me, poking through my sock. Thankfully, the adrenaline coursing through me dampened the pain. I forced myself to slow despite the way my pounding heart said *run, run, run!* with every beat. If I gave myself away now by making too much noise, I probably wouldn't get a second chance.

Where even was I? It looked like Walter had broken into someone's home who was gone for the holidays, but that didn't give me any clues and I couldn't stay hidden forever. As silently as I could, I shifted my weight and blew on my hands to ward off the cold. I couldn't stay in one place for long, and my chances of being found would rise with the sun. I had to keep moving, but—

The snap of branches sounded from my left, and I pressed myself against a tree.

My eyes hadn't fully adjusted to the night after the brightness inside the house, and my pounding heart felt like it was announcing my presence to anyone nearby.

I held my breath and pressed back harder so the tree's rough bark poked through my sweater.

I'd made too much noise while running. I should have been more careful. But how had he caught up to me so fast? If the pepper spray hadn't stopped him, I figured the kick to his groin would have.

I chewed on my nail and tried to blink back tears. If he caught me again—

A hand wrapped around my arm.

I screamed and tried to twist away.

"It's me," a soft voice said, as he wrapped his other arm around my middle in a steadying embrace. "Harp, it's me."

I collapsed against Seb, burying my head against his chest as my legs threatened to give out.

Somehow, he'd found me.

Chapter 18

Best Christmas Ever

"I've got you," Seb murmured against my hair as he tightened his arms around my middle.

The sound of the police rushing the house and my captor's angry cries filled the air, but I mashed my cheek against Seb's solid chest and forced it all away, breathing in his musky scent. Everything felt distant, like I was watching the scene unfold through a foggy window.

"It's okay. You're okay now." He ran one hand up and down my back in long, comforting strokes while the other stayed around my waist.

And with Seb here, things did finally feel okay.

In the background, the sounds of a struggle and a single shot cracked the night's silence, but I just gripped Seb tighter. He didn't move, so neither did I.

After a few minutes of being held in his strong arms, my shaking receded enough that I finally asked, "What are you doing here?"

"I came with the police to help find you. I was supposed to stay in the car, but..."

His words warmed my heart, but I shook my head, scraping my nose against his wool coat. "No, I mean how did you know I was here?"

"Remember how I set up those security cameras around your house once we realized you were being followed?"

"Yeah."

"One of them caught the license plate of the guy's car when he drove off with you." His voice tightened to match his hug. "And we used that to track the car here."

"You saved me," I said softly.

"I didn't do anything. It was the police who tracked you here." He sighed. "I never should've left you alone in the first place. I—"

"Did you find her, Sebastian?" another male voice called.

"Yes, we're over here," Seb called back, his voice a low rumble in his chest.

The crack of twigs announced Sheriff Warner's arrival. "Good. We've got the suspect in custody."

"What's going to happen?" I asked the sheriff. Despite the security of Seb's arms around me, my voice trembled.

"Since he kidnapped you, we can lock him up with those charges, but considering he had a gun on him, I'm confident that ballistics will prove the gun was the one that shot Tom Stevens." Sheriff Warner rubbed his hands together, either from the cold or anticipation. "With this evidence and the testimony of the man we arrested, it should be a fairly open and shut case."

"Tate is going to testify against Walter?" I shuddered.

"I guess he received a threatening note from the killer about Tom's death," Sheriff Warner said.

No wonder Tate had been so freaked.

The next half hour passed in a blur. Soon I was back at the police station, sitting in a small room, with a blanket wrapped around my shoulders, a mug of cocoa in one hand, and Seb holding the other.

A knock sounded on the door, and Tate walked in a moment later.

I stiffened and tightened my grip on Seb's hand.

"Harp, I'm so sorry." Tate rushed over but stopped at a look Seb gave him. "You have no idea how terrible I've felt since I found out what happened."

I stared at him, trying to figure out what to say, but he plowed on.

"I didn't mean to drag you into all this."

Seb's clenched jaw matched the pressure of his grip on my hand.

"Why didn't you just pay him?" I whispered once I found my voice again.

"I didn't have the money." Tate paced the room with short, agitated steps, not looking at me. "I never told you this, but I got into gambling trouble our last year of college, and it's ruined me."

I blinked up at him as so many things fell into place. Tate's late nights out. His inability to pay his car loan. His sudden aloofness.

"I borrowed money to pay off some of the debts, but it didn't cover everything. When Ashley mentioned you'd inherited your grandmother's shop, I figured some money might've come with it, so I came to ask, but I never imagined he'd follow me here." Tate hung his head.

For once, I didn't even grimace at the mention of my cheating roommate.

"And how did Tom get mixed up in this?" Seb asked.

Tate frowned and looked at me. "Didn't you recognize him? He was in my fraternity."

"No, I didn't." But now that he said it, it made sense that Tom had asked if we'd met before. Still though, what were the chances that Tom and I would both end up in Whisper Hollow after all these years?

"I got him into gambling, and he ran off when his debts got too bad." Tate's gaze flicked to me, then away again. "I came here for you, but also because Tom was here."

"And that's how you met Helen?"

He swallowed but must've decided there was no reason to lie anymore. "Yes. She knew about Tom's gambling and decided to help me get with you since we all needed money to pay off our debts."

Helen had lied to us after all. I flashed a look at Seb, whose lips were pressed into a firm line.

"But the next thing I knew, Tom was dead." Tate swallowed. "That's when I realized that Walter had followed me here, but no one believed me until it was too late, and he'd already taken you." Tate closed his eyes briefly, then looked at me once more. "It was lucky one of the officers brought me my phone or who knows what might've happened..."

"You never should have embroiled Harper in your crap." Seb's eyes flashed.

"I'm sorry," Tate said. "I just came to say that and to let you know that I'm leaving town."

"That's for the best." I pulled the blanket tighter around me. "I don't want to see you again."

"I understand." He turned to go.

"I'm serious, Tate," I said before he made it to the door. "You didn't listen to me before, but if you do something like this again, I'll get a restraining order." I wouldn't put up with his stalker crap again—not after everything else he'd put me through.

The door shut behind him with a satisfying click, and for the first time in forever, there was no part of me missing Tate. He was a chapter in my life I could finally close the book on.

It was time for something new.

I turned to Seb, my pants rustling on the bench's plastic top.

"Not going to lie, I was about ready to cheer when you threatened him with a restraining order." He gave me a crooked grin, revealing my favorite dimple.

My poor, battered heart started pounding again. "Seb, I—"

"Wait." He held up a hand and handed me my phone. "You should talk to your sister. She's been freaking out."

Grace. How could I have forgotten about her?

I stared down at the phone as weariness pressed in on me. As soon as I heard her voice, I was sure to fall apart again.

"A text should be fine for now," Seb said, as if reading my mind.

"Right. A text." I exhaled in relief, then typed out a quick message to Grace, promising her I was all right, the guy had been caught, and I'd call her in the morning.

As I hit send, Seb cleared his throat and said, "You might want to send one to Nancy and María too. They've also been pretty worried."

I groaned but did as he requested. "Does the whole town know?"

Seb grinned. "Knowing Nancy, that's a distinct possibility."

I frowned. Once Nancy realized Walter was the killer, she was going to be so disappointed. I was pretty sure she had a thing for Walter.

"How long was I gone?"

"About six hours." His grin flickered out as quickly as a broken Christmas light.

"It felt like a lot longer than that." I took another sip of my cocoa, which wasn't nearly as good as Nancy's but at least it was warm.

"Yes, it did."

His low murmur made my pulse race. "How did you find out?"

"Once your call disconnected, Grace called 911, then she called Nancy, who called María and me to fill us in."

"And that's when you rushed over and told the police about the security footage?"

"Exactly."

"My hero." I sighed and leaned my head against his shoulder.

Seb pressed a soft kiss against the top of my head that made my heart skip a beat. "If that were true, I never would've let you get taken in the first place." His voice cracked, and he cleared his throat.

I straightened and faced him on the bench, taking in the tired lines around his eyes and his hair standing on end like he'd run his hands through it too many times. "Seb, that wasn't your fault. We thought the danger was gone, and I was the one who asked you to leave."

"Even if the danger was gone, I shouldn't have left like that, not without telling you how I feel." He exhaled slowly, then met my gaze. "I've regretted it since the moment I drove away."

"You did?" My heartbeat picked up speed again.

"Yeah." He turned so we more fully faced each other and put our cocoa down on the bench before taking both my hands in his. "I kind of messed things up by asking to be your fake boyfriend, but I couldn't stand the thought of you dating Tate again, not when you should be dating me."

Was this really happening?

"But you apologized for kissing me," I whispered. "Twice."

He sighed and ran a hand through his already messy hair. "I apologized because I shouldn't have kissed you when you thought it was fake. I wanted our first kiss to be more than a show we put on for anyone else." He squeezed my hand. "It felt like I was taking advantage of you somehow since none of it was fake for me."

"I thought you just wanted to be friends." Tears pricked at my eyes.

"I do want to be friends." He leaned in and pressed a soft kiss to my forehead before meeting my gaze again. "These last few months, you've become one of my best friends, Harp. But I also want to be more than that. I want to be the one who makes you smile, who holds you when you're scared, and who kisses away your tears. But when you told me you wanted to go back to just being friends, I didn't think I could tell you without pushing my feelings on you and that was the last thing I wanted after everything you'd been through with Tate."

I stared at him. Was this real, or some sort of strange, sweet Christmas dream to counter the nightmare I'd just gone through?

"I'm sorry that I went about this all wrong." He sighed but didn't let go of my hands. "I never should've started the fake relationship."

"No." I shook my head slowly. "It's good you did. I think I would've been too scared to be with you for real. At least at first. But spending all that time together helped me realize the truth."

"Which is?" He stilled.

"It wasn't fake for me either."

He put a hand on my cheek, and I leaned into his touch. "So does this mean you'll be my girlfriend for real?"

I met his hopeful gaze and smiled. For so long, I'd been terrified of getting hurt again; of opening myself up to a relationship and letting someone disappoint me the way Tate had. But now I knew it was the vulnerability that made relationships worthwhile. If you only held people at arm's length and never opened yourself up to the chance of being hurt, you never fully let them in and experienced the joy either.

"That depends," I said with a small smile. "If we're dating for real, does that mean there's no need to practice kissing?"

"I wouldn't go that far." His expression melted into a smolder, and he leaned down until his lips were just above mine. "You know what they say, practice makes perfect."

He brushed a strand of hair behind my ear, his gentle touch leaving a trail of heat on my skin. His lips met mine in a tender, yet passionate kiss. The station around us faded, leaving only the warmth of his touch, and the promise in his eyes, and my heart that raced a little too fast. His hand cupped the curve of my jaw, his thumb tracing a soft line up and down the side of my neck.

"Best Christmas ever," I murmured against his mouth.

He smiled and kissed me again.

Chapter 19

New Year's Resolutions

"Are you sure you aren't going to regret this?" I asked Seb in the car a few days later as we pulled into my sister's driveway.

"You do realize that's like the fifth time you've asked me that since we got off the plane," Seb teased with a grin. He kept one hand on the wheel of the rental car and took mine in his other.

I blew out a breath. "I guess I'm just nervous. My family can be a lot sometimes." And since my parents were also visiting Grace for the holidays, this was sort of a big deal. Ready or not, Seb was getting the whole family.

"It'll be fine." Seb squeezed my hand, then pulled into Grace's driveway. "It can't be any worse than your introduction to *my* family."

The fact that he could joke about Cooper, combined with the Christmas package we mailed off before we left, proved he was moving forward.

"Besides, Grace and I have been texting a bit and I feel like I have a pretty good idea of her personality now."

I narrowed my eyes. "You've been texting my sister? What about?"

"You, of course." He smirked. "I've been charged with sending her daily updates of how you're doing, if you're eating properly, who else has been asking you out, what time you—"

"Shut up. You were not." I laughed but then stopped. That actually did sound like something Grace might ask for, especially after the whole kidnapping incident. She'd been way overprotective. Not that I could blame her. I still had a hard time being alone after what had happened. My own house didn't feel safe anymore. "And for the record, no one asked me out but Loren, so stop making it sound like there's this huge list."

Seb shook his head. "Poor Loren. If he wasn't my competition, I'd almost feel sorry for the guy."

I leaned over and gave him a quick kiss on the cheek. "Trust me, you don't have any competition."

Almost as soon as Seb parked, my five nieces and nephews streamed from the house and surrounded the car, pressing their faces against the windows.

Seb blanched. "They're like little zombies. Are you sure it's safe to go out there?"

I laughed again. "I thought you were ready for this."

"I am." He set his jaw and met my eyes. "More than you know."

We opened our doors, and the next few minutes passed in a whirlwind of hugs and greetings as we fought through the swarm of children to get into the house.

"It's so good to have you home." Mom pulled me to the couch.

We chatted for a while, and I kept one eye on Seb and the kids as they forced him to play Legos, dolls, some variation of Red Light, Green Light and Red Rover. I should have intervened and saved him, but watching him interact with them was too adorable.

Grace came over with a smile. "I'll admit, I'm impressed. He's already memorized all the kids' names."

"He's a keeper," I said, echoing Nancy's words from so long ago.

"Now *that* I'd agree with." Grace gave me a sneaky smile.

"What?" I shrugged.

"So, no more fake dating?" she asked as Mom came back bearing cups of eggnog.

"Nope, this is for real." I took a sip of the sweet, creamy drink and smiled at Seb as he whispered something to the kids. They all glanced at me, their smiles widening.

Grace watched me until I turned and met her gaze. "What about the chances of getting hurt?"

"It's just like Nana used to say." I smiled. "Every big story requires a big leap of faith. And for Seb, that's a risk I'm willing to take."

~ The End ~

The mystery may be solved, but one question remains: What did you think of the story? Your review can help other readers crack the case of deciding their next cozy mystery read. Please write a review (even just one line) or leave a rating/review on <u>Amazon</u>, <u>Goodreads</u>, or <u>Bookbub</u>.

<u>Join my mailing list </u>and receive Harper and Sebastian character art.

To find out what happens next in Harper's story, read
<u>Murder With a Hint of Dark Chocolate</u>.

About the author

Laura M. Drake grew up in Arkansas before attending Brigham Young University to become a teacher. After working for a few years, she moved to Tokyo and fell in love with writing. She produces clean stories that readers of any age can enjoy. When she isn't writing, she enjoys reading, playing ultimate frisbee and board games, and spending time with her family and friends. Laura is a member of The Church Of Jesus Christ of Latter-day Saints.

Use this QR code or the hyperlink to get to Laura M. Drake's linktree, which has links to her social media, books, and a free short story.

Check out
Laura M. Drake

Also by

The Chronicles of Andar — a YA trilogy where Harry Potter meets
Avatar: the Last Airbender

Japanese Haunting — a clean spooky series that's perfect for fall

Till Life Do Us Part — a paranormal romantic suspense standalone

One Dark Night — a collection of short mysteries that's perfect for an
eerie read

<u>Once Upon a Raven</u> — a collection of fairytale retellings with a twist

Afterword

Thank you for joining me in Whisper Hollow once again. If you enjoyed Murder With a Hint of Peppermint please leave a rating/review on <u>Amazon,</u> <u>Goodreads,</u> or <u>Bookbub</u>. Also be sure to check out <u>Murder With a Hint of Dark Chocolate</u> to find out what happens next with Harper.

Book Club Questions

1. Did the festive holiday atmosphere add to or detract from the story's tension?

2. Were there any holiday traditions in the book that resonated with you? How did they add to the mystery or the romance?

3. What did you think of the fake dating trope in this story? How did it affect the characters' growth and the resolution?

4. How did the presence of the ex-fiancé shape the main character's emotional journey and the story's conflict?

5. Forgiveness is a central theme in this book. What would you have done in the character's place?

6. Which character did you relate to most? Did any character surprise you?

7. Were there any clues or red herrings that threw you off or made the mystery more compelling? Did you guess the cul-

prit?

8. How did the small-town community play a role in the unfolding of the story? Did you enjoy the gossip and interconnected relationships?

9. What was your favorite scene in the book? Was it more focused on the mystery, the romance, or the holiday spirit?

10. Do you agree with how forgiveness was portrayed? Was it more for the forgiver's peace or the forgiven's redemption?

11. How did the fake dating arrangement evolve into something real? Were any turning points particularly poignant, funny, or frustrating?

12. What makes this book a quintessential cozy mystery for you? Did it hit all the elements you expected?

13. Did the ending resolve all your questions? If not, what loose threads would you have liked to see tied up?

14. Compare this book to other books you have read by Laura M. Drake or other books you have read covering the same or similar themes. How are they the same or different?

15. Did you highlight or bookmark any passages from the book? Did you have a favorite quote or quotes? If so, share which and why.

Check out
Laura M. Drake

Printed in Great Britain
by Amazon

54571828R10118